…ishes
David 7.97.

# A Kind of HEAVEN

stories

David Almond

David Almond.

IRON PRESS

First Published 1997 by IRON Press
5, Marden Terrace, Cullercoats,
North Shields, Northumberland NE30 4PD, UK
Tel/Fax: (0191) 253 1901

Typeset by David Stephenson
in Palatino 9.5 point

Printed by Peterson Printers
South Shields



Book design by Peter Mortimer
Cover design by Michael Adam

ISBN 0–906228–62-X

The following stories were first published as detailed:
*Instead of the Scheme* and *Fiesta*: Iron
*1962*:Stand
*A Kind of Heaven* and *Beacon Hill*: Panurge
*Where Your Wings Were*: Radio 4
*Nesting*: Northern Stories 1 (Littlewood Press)
*After the Abandoned Wharves*: Northern Stories 2 (Littlewood Press)
*Dogs*: Raven
*Spotlight*: The Page
*Lucy Blue*: Northern Electric News

NORTHERN Arts

*IRON Press books are represented by:*
*Password Books Ltd*
*23 New Mount Street*
*Manchester M4 4DE*
*Tel: (0161) 953 4009*
*Fax: (0161) 953 4001*
*E-mail: password-books@ncr1.poptel.org.uk*

*for Sara Jane*

# *The Stories*

# A Kind of Heaven

Why had he been so scared? She seemed well, that morning they left the house above the beach, headed to the city, the day he encountered Harris for the first time.

Icy and bright. The sun rising. Threads of frost in the ribbed sand. The sea like burnished metal, an almost imperceptible swell.

She burst in on him, dragged him from his bed, held him at the window.

"Such a day," she said. "Look at the glow in it. Look at the shine from it. And you in bed. You and him both in bed."

As he dressed, through the open doors he heard her counting coins into her purse, heard her laughing with his father. "Stuffy thing," she called him. "Old misery." He heard them struggling together on the bed, their exclamations of effort and pain, their joy, her cry,

"Tom, rescue me! Tom, come and rescue me."

The father, in his dressing gown, chased them from the house and they ran out hand in hand onto the road above the beach. They halted there, stood pulling on their coats and scarves.

"Old misery!" she called. "We're well rid of you, old man!"

From the gate he shook his fist at her.

"Of you and all!" he yelled. "Of you and him and all!"

They took the bus to Newcastle, headed down towards the quay.

The city was silent, but for the footsteps of the others going down with them, their raised voices and laughter. She was in scarlet, the skirt of her coat swinging against him with every step. He kept watching her, checking her, then turning to the others, waiting for them to be drawn by her. They were on Dean Street, steep curve of massive buildings, Victorian and black, leading to the river shining from below. Above their heads, the platform of the bridge headed out dead straight between the roofs, the arch stretched into the sky.

Sunday. Market day. Rows of stalls between the warehouses; narrow, white-canopied alleyways filled with the smell of meat frying, the voices of crowds and stallholders, music pouring from transistors - tunes left over from the war, skiffle and Presley, the Beatles' wail. She held a shirt against him, mused, shook her head. She lifted dresses and hats towards herself, posed for him. "This?" she asked. "Or this one? Does it do anything for me?" She laid it all back on the stalls - "Tat," she called it. "Nothing but tat." - and bought only a singlet for her husband, with, "Poor soul. Needs the warmth these days. Needs a bit of caring." Outside the alleyways, they stood at the water's edge. She smeared mustard onto hot beef sandwiches and they stood pressed close together by the passing crowd, laughing at the unwieldiness of the food, catching the juices with their tongues. And they groaned with pleasure, cleaned each other with her handkerchief, kissed each other.

Outside the canopies, a crowd had gathered at the foot of a crane. She pulled him to it, stood on tiptoe, peered through.

"No!" she gasped. "Never! No!"

"What is it?" he demanded, straining to see, failing. "What's happening?"

She laughed at his confusion.

"In there, look. In the middle, Tom."

"I see nothing."

"It's Harris. Little Harris has returned."

And she took his hand, led him through towards the centre.

Harris was short, squat, naked to the waist. There were blurred tattoos on his skin, dozens of little nicks and bruises. He had a small sack hooked to the tip of a cane. He thrust it out at the spectators, glared at them.

"Get your money out," he told them. "There's nothing to be seen till you pay."

Behind him, a cartwheel rested against the crane. There was a knapsack, a heap of chains and locks, a blanket opened out to reveal a range of needles and pins and skewers.

Tom looked at her, nudged her.

"Watch," she said. "Just watch and wait."

Harris saw them, newcomers, thrust his sack at them.

"Get your money out," he said. "There's nothing to see till you pay."

As she dropped in her pennies he glared at Tom, fixed him with his stare.

"For him and all," he said. "The squirt there. Make sure you've paid for him and all."

They waited. Time after time he thrust the sack into the crowd. He kept pulling it back, counting the coins in there, peering back at the spectators with disappointed eyes, telling them, "Not for this, oh no. Risk so much for this?" And he'd come at them again, each time louder in his demands, each time more pugnacious, and Tom in his frustration kept asking her,

"How long? How long's he going to take?"

"An age," she told him. "Always an age. Some days we'd stand an hour or more and see nothing but his yelling and stamping his feet. Good to see him. I thought he'd moved on, died even. Harris. Little Harris. After all these years."

Behind them the crowd had increased. They were being shuffled forward, the space around Harris was diminishing. He leaned into the crowd, stretched his arm out across their shoulders, demanded payment from the back. From somewhere catcalls and whistling had started.

"Impatient, eh?" he shouted. "Want the show started, eh? Then get your cash out. Pay your way. Nothing's for nothing."

And Tom sighed.

"Do something," he whispered, gripping his mother's hand tight. "Drop the sack and do something."

Harris at last recoiled from his audience. He held up a few coins, as if he were in despair. He laid the cane and sack on the ground. He lifted the cartwheel onto its rim, rolled it until it was upright in front of him. He lifted it, a few inches, let it drop to the ground and Tom felt the concrete shuddering beneath his feet.

"Best timber," said Harris. "Best steel. Listen." And he lifted it again, dropped it again. "Some body in it, eh?"

He stood watching, taking deep breaths, blowing out air, sucking it in. The watchers were still being pressed forward by those at the back. He cried out as he lifted the wheel, and it stilled them all. He lifted it in one movement, leaned his head back, rested the rim on his brow. He stamped, settling himself, then took his hands from the wheel and left it resting there. He took little steps, he held his arms out wide, kept adjusting himself as the wheel threatened to fall. The muscles in his neck stretched and bulged, his cries were strangled in his throat. The crowd edged back now, scared that the wheel would fall. Someone was giggling, others were yelling, urging him on. His mother held Tom tight. She was smiling. "Nothing changes," she said. "Still the same." Soon Harris reached up to the wheel again, lifted it free, rested it in front of him. Released from the weight, he jumped several times, then stared out. There were tears in his eyes, little pieces of dirt and grit were embedded in his brow.

"Poor Harris," she whispered. "Poor soul."

"The wheel," he said. "The wheel. What's next? Who wants to chain Harris? Who wants to lock the chains round his throat and his limbs and say, there Harris, no getting out of that? Eh? Eh? Or the needles. The pins and needles sticking out?" He came at the crowd, glaring, thrusting his face at them. "Get your loot out. Get your money out and pay." He lifted the cane and the sack. "Give," he demanded. "Get giving." He muscled his way into the crowd. "You," he said. "And you. You haven't paid. You haven't. And you and all."

The crowd began to disperse. Many of those at the front turned back towards the stalls, letting those at the back come through. Tom was being drawn away by his mother. "He'll make us wait an age for this," she said. He followed her towards the water's edge. They headed for the bridge. From behind came Harris' calling. "Where you going? Why you leaving? You and all. Always something else to see." Tom turned, saw Harris standing outside the crowd now. Harris caught his eye, beckoned to him. "Squirt!" he yelled. "And you! That pretty one! Where you off to? Why?"

She pulled Tom on. She was laughing. "Don't look back," she said. "Or he'll never let you get away." The river ran a dozen feet below them. There were gulls screaming, riding the gentle breezes at the river's centre.

"Harris," she said. "Fancy. Little Harris. Your father should have come."

"Who is he?"

"He was in Egypt with your father. Came back with him, on the same boat home. Poor soul. He'd had too much. The war, the heat.

They'd got to him."

In the shade beneath the bridge, they caught their breath. The air was bitter, frost remained. They waited at the foot of the bridge's stone column, waiting for the lift to come. She drew him into the shelter formed by the massive curves of steel descending to meet the quay. Leaning back, feeling the huge rivets of the bridge pressing on his spine, he watched her shudder, watched her fasten tight the scarlet collar at her throat.

"Damned place," she said, and the laughter had left her eyes, her voice was trembling. "So bitter cold. Keeps on telling me he'll take us off to the pyramids for a winter, make us miss all this. Cairo. Do you believe it?"

The lift came. A little man on a stool inside the door escorted them. Tom saw how the man watched her, how he couldn't take his eyes off her.

"Madam," the man said after the ascent, holding back the steel gates for her. "And young sir as well." She dropped a coin into a box on the wall. "So kind. Thank you, madam."

She giggled, stepping out, gasped at the wind that was blowing freely here. She started running, took Tom's hand and dashed towards the centre of the bridge. She leaned over the parapet, he peered through its rails, saw her face filling the sky, hair streaming in the wind. She leaned further, further, till her head was inverted, almost level with his own, and she laughed, "Hold me, Tom! Keep me back!" And in terror he swivelled and clutched her, both arms around the knees.

"Silly thing," she said. "Silly thing. I couldn't fall."

She crouched by him, held her arm across the parapet, showed him the warehouses packing the wharves, the tangle of cranes stretching east towards the sea. Half a mile away a white liner was docked.

"Maybe that'd take us," she said. "Maybe that'd get us somewhere away from this."

Her hair swept across his throat. The wind whipped away her scent, her breath. Her voice mingled with the screaming of the gulls. He lowered his head, stared through the gaps towards the quay: neat arrangement of white canopies and stalls, slowly-moving crowd. Beneath the crane he saw the tight circle of spectators with Harris at their centre. He was a tiny tortured figure, jerking and squirming on the ground.

"Look," he said.

"The chains," she said. "The locks and chains."

And he wanted to ask her more, but suddenly she was away, and he couldn't catch her, and she was yelling,

"Race you to the other side!"

They held each other tight, returning. The platform of the bridge led them straight towards the city's heart. All around, on road and pavement and the bridge's steel, frost was forming, sparkling in the brilliant late light. When he raised his head, he was astonished to see a pale moon already hanging over the roofs and spires and stacks.

"But of course," she chided. "Short days, Tom. Winter. Early nights."

And as they left the bridge, entered the city's streets, the sky began to change, streaks of colour began to gather in the west. They spread and deepened, made the emptiness above them bleed and flame.

"What will become of us?" she sighed, stopping at a newspaper seller's stall, looking down at Kruschev with his fists raised, at headlines demanding that the bomb tests must go on, we must always be prepared, we mustn't hesitate. "No time since men were exhausted or made mad by it all, since they came back telling us never, never again."

The newspaper seller held out his cupped palm, muttered curses, then yelled after them as they moved away.

"No good running off! It's coming soon! It'll catch you soon!"

"Yes, it's coming," she whispered, and the boy had to strain to hear her. "It'll come again."

In the dimly-lit station, waiting at their bay, they leaned towards each other, stamped their feet, kept exclaiming at the cold, kept laughing, breaking into little jigs.

"This'll be it," they cried at each new set of headlights appearing in the streets outside. "No, the next one... the next but one."

Outside, on the monument, the angel stood as always, poised for flight above the heap of fighting men.

"When I count to thirty," she said. "One, two..."

"No, ten!"

And he rushed into his counting, till eight, when he left a massive gulf till nine, then started out again with,

"Nine and one millionth... nine and two millionths..."

"Fool!" she said, and she cuffed him, the woollen-gloved hand falling gently across his cheek. "Millionths!"

The fire in the sky faded, the moon became bright. He pointed out the stars he'd learned from his father on the pitch black beach.

"The Archer," he said. He traced it, followed its pattern with his outstretched arm. She crouched, her head level with his, allowing him to show her.

"His belt, you see. His bow, his arm drawn back. The arrow's tip."

"Oh, yes," she said. "I think I see."

He laughed. "You don't," he said. "Not that quick. Course you don't." He nudged her, and she grinned at him. "It's hard," he said. "But once you see, it's easy. You'll see him standing there night after night after night."

"It's all made up, of course," he said, when they were standing, jigging again. "His stars have got nothing to do with each other. It's just the way they look to us, from where we are in everything."

The bus arrived at last. They sat huddled on the long back seat.

"He'll think we've run away," she said, and she giggled. "He'll think we've found a handsome rich devil to take us away from this."

"He'll think we've been kidnapped. He'll think they've got us in a dark cellar somewhere and want a fortune to give us back."

"He'll think: Thank God - I'm rid of those two brats."

"They're off my back at last."

"He's in for a shock, then, eh?"

The bus rattled out from the city. He kept turning to her, stealing glances. It made her laugh. "Who d'you think you're looking at?" she asked, turning to the window, haughty. She was well, so well. In the blackness beyond the streetlights the boy slept against her. In his dream, Harris crouched half-naked in the frost beneath the bridge. He was wrapped in chains, padlocked, the nicks on his body were fresh wounds trickling with blood. Behind him, far beyond the river and the city's fringes, the horizon was aflame: real fire raging to the sky. "Squirt," he whispered. "You. Squirt." He sneered at the boy's mother, fixed the boy with his eye. "Her an all," he whispered. "The red-coated one, that pretty one, her an all."

He woke to her talking of food, what would be waiting for them.

"...hot stew with little crisp dumplings. The house filled with the smell of it, everywhere heated by the oven and the fire all day long. Carrots cut longways with that buttery coating of his, spinach bright green and oh so tender to cut. Can you imagine it, Tom? Can you taste it?"

He buried his face in her coat, let her words move Harris from his mind.

"...warm honey seeping from the warm cake, mingling with the white sauce... licking your lips to catch every last drop of it, holding it on your tongue a moment more, a moment more..."

In their village they descended from the bus to find his father rushing out of the darkness at them.

"Where've you been?" he demanded. "Where've you bloody been?"

And they hurried home, laughing at the unevenness of the lane above the beach, gripping each other tight each time another stumbled. She kept talking of Harris, little Harris, poor Harris.

"Poor Harris!" said her husband. "He's a wild man. Should've stayed out with the snake charmers and the dervishes. Had his brains boiled - too much sun, too many magic men..."

Inside, the rooms were as warm as she'd anticipated. They ate small pasties hot from the oven, with carrots as she'd said and potatoes whipped into a cream. Afterwards there was rice, creamy and sweet beneath its scorched skin.

Much later, Tom opened his eyes, looked out from his bed to see the Archer poised above the sea. He heard waves slapping at the rocks, and as he fell asleep again, heard his parents murmuring their pleasure in the night...

"Trickery, nothing more. War brought them out. Charlatans from Cairo's cellars. Brought them heading up from the desert with their antics and their potions and their hands held out. A higher form of begging, nothing more. They'd squat there in the squares stroking cobras. They'd have swords rammed down their throats, nails in their nostrils. They'd chain themselves into bags and boxes and nets and they'd lie sunk for minutes at a time in tanks of filthy water. Sorcery? They were wild men, crazed men. Who knows what they took that bubbled through their blood? They wouldn't sit in the corners patient and abject like the others, with their deliberately-severed limbs and their eyes burned out. They had to perform, had to confront you, had to pursue you if you turned away. You, mister! You pay, mister! Glaring at you, eyes wild, brains boiled, scuttling down the alleys after you. Pay, mister! You pay!"

They were on the beach, on the firm sand left by the ebbing tide. Fishing boats, surrounded by gulls, headed in from the horizon. They walked slowly north, towards the headland, past coal gatherers knee-deep in the water with their sieves, separating black fragments of coal from the beige sand. At the water's edge stood the ponies and carts, the stuffed sacks. The beach narrowed, became a thin strip bounded by water on one side, tank traps left from the war on the other. Another bright day, the sun on its low trajectory through an unblemished sky.

Tom kept turning to his father, wanting the silence to be broken again.

"Harris believed it all, you see. He told us these people had conquered something in themselves. He said they felt no pain, that they had no desires. He believed that their contortions and their scars were signs that they had disciplined themselves, that they had risen above the world. He was there too long. The heat, the war. He fell for it, for all of it. Your mother's right. Poor Harris. Poor bloody Harris. What was the pain he wanted to blot out? I remember on the boat, all of us sitting round him, the first time I saw him with the needles, running them through the lighter flame then sticking them in all over himself. At each needle he shuts his eyes a moment, a little gasp, opens them again with a light shining there like he's proud, so proud, like he's knowing something none of the audience'll never know. And all the time the guys giggling and nudging each other and going, That's right, Harris, get the buggers in, until he starts whispering and we all close down and hear him going, Nothing, nothing, nothing. And in the end he gets this skewer, one of them we've eaten lumps of meat off and he starts shoving it in through his cheek right where the jawbone is and pushing further with the blood trickling so we can hardly bear to go on watching. And those that do watch see the skewer coming out the other cheek, pressing the skin out to a point until it bursts through and the blood's running down his other cheek now and the point's coming further out, and his eyes are tight shut, tight shut, till finally he opens them again and he's looking out at us but like he sees none of us, and some of us get close and stare deep and see the skewer right across the entrance to his throat, and all the time he's sighing, sighing, sighing. Just like the sighs a man makes when he loves... Harris. Once the boat docked, thought I'd seen the last of him. Till down on the quay one Sunday with your mother and she says, What's going on here? And I look through the crowd and there he is, yelling, Pay! Get your bloody money out! It's Harris, I say, It's bloody Harris. And I push through to him, wondering will he know me, and I stand right in front of him but all he does is jab me with his money bag, and tell me, For her an all, that pretty one, for her an all, and sees nothing in me, remembers nothing of me. Harris. I'll have to see him. Thought he'd've moved on by now. Thought he'd be dead by now..."

At the headland they squatted on the rocks. The water sucked and spat, draining through ancient channels, leaving the pools, brilliant pools filled with the deep blueness of sky, that held within themselves bright weeds and mosses, unfolding anemones. They lifted rocks, laughed at the crabs scuttling back into cover, the tiny fish that dashed into the weed. Once Tom plunged his hand deep into a pool, took out a crab, held it between thumb and forefinger, while the legs waved and the claws snapped uselessly. He placed his fingertip inside a claw, let it grip him, and he giggled: it was just a tickling, that was all.

They turned back, headed home. Small gusts of wind swept dry sand inches-high across the wet sand. It tingled at their ankles. Inland, they saw frost in the depressions in the dunes, and twenty miles away snow lay covering the Cheviots. His mother was out, tiny green-clothed figure waving from the gate and calling them. Tom waved back, leaping high and swinging his arms above his head.

Closer to home, his father asked quietly,

"How was she, on Sunday in town?"

Tom stared.

"Energetic? Able to take a day of it?"

Tom nodded.

"Course she was," he said. "You should have seen her, running full pelt on the bridge."

There'd be places with little pain. He'd been told that. At school they'd drawn maps of their hands. Tom had closed his eyes while his friend Askew touched the skin with the needle's point. "Where am I touching now?" said Askew. "What can you feel now?" And it was true. There were places almost without sensation, where Askew could press harder, and Tom would hear the smile in his voice as he asked, "Nothing, eh? And here? And now?" Together they mapped the points of pain and the points of nothingness, and then Tom sat gazing down at the pinpricks on his skin while the teacher asked, "So what have we learned from this? What conclusions can be drawn? Why are some parts of us more sensitive than other parts..?"

He repeated the exercise now, in the solitude of his room. It was dusk, the Archer was forming, he heard the sea sliding across the sand, coming in. He sat at the bed's edge, bare-chested, closing his eyes each time he touched his body with the point. Where was he touching now? And now? He tried to separate himself from the knowledge of what his hand and arm were doing. This was impossible. He knew he was both donor and receiver of the pain. But still there were moments when he doubted this, when he had to open his eyes and see that the needle was indeed being pressed into his skin; and moments when his hand recoiled and he gasped at the intensity of what had been intended as a gentle touch.

He pulled on his shirt, dropped the needle when he heard them coming up. He listened. How slow was she? What help did she need? She'd slept most of the evening downstairs, after complaining of the cold, the damned cold. Tom had stared at his father. It was nothing, he'd been told. Nothing. They watched TV together in silence. Every half hour there came news of war, the cold war. Again and again they saw Kruschev storming out, saying it couldn't go on, the treaties must end. Once they caught each other's eye, half in panic, when she suddenly gasped in her sleep, drew her knees to her chest, but when she woke at last she'd been dreaming of Derwent Water, of waking early, looking out across the still water towards Catbells and Skiddaw. The honeymoon, the story Tom knew so well: bus journey through the Pennines to the Lakes; the Lodore; how had they been able to afford it?; walking out as if into their kingdom; the fells and water; the rocky summits; sunlight; joy; world's rebirth. He listened again as they drew from their memories images that were so familiar to him that they might almost have been authentic memories of his own, were it not for the fact that only two of them existed then, only two of them walked hand in hand there, only two of them were reunited, released at last from war. And for the first time Tom understood his isolation, his exclusion from them. The heaven they described was theirs, and could exist only in memory, in the years between the war's end and his birth.

"Tom?" she'd said, reaching out to him. "Tom?"

He sat stiffly, feeling her eyes on him.

"What is it, Tom?"

He shrugged. His eyes were burning. He motioned to the TV.

"Why do they call it that?" he asked. "Why do they say the war is cold?"

They hadn't been able to answer him. He'd kissed them, come upstairs.

He listened. They whispered, they sighed. He heard what sounded like her sudden cry of pain. There was a knock at his door, his father entered.

"Still sitting up, I see."

"The stars. Just watching."

"Ah. No windows open, have you?"

"No."

"We'll close the curtains, though. So cold. Draughts everywhere."

Leaving, he hesitated at the door.

"Probably come to nothing, you know. We've had it before, all this threatening, sabre-rattling. What we'll do and what we won't do to each other. My bomb's bigger than your bomb. It's a game, son, just a bloody game."

"Probably."

"It's sick. But we'll survive." He leaned down, touched the boy's shoulder. "Whatever happens, we'll survive. Yes?"

Tom looked up, but his tongue was stilled by unaskable, unanswerable questions.

"Yes," said his father. "Yes. Yes, yes, yes."

Afterwards, when there was only the sound of their regular breathing and the waves were washing the sand, Tom dropped from his bed to crawl on hands and knees, seeking the needle, but it was nowhere. When he slept, he felt the massive rivets of the bridge pressing on his spine. They were bending him, forming him. Where was she? He scanned the quays. He stretched high, but all was silent, deserted. The river was metallic, the sun glared from the middle of the sky. He kept on growing, he arched, stretched from quay to quay with the river far below him. Then he saw her, tiny, scarlet-coated. She stood at the parapet, smiling, then ran, turned, ran again. She ran full pelt with her coat tails flying, running and turning, held within him, safe.

He went again, this time with his father. She saw their reluctance to leave her, but she scorned their fears. "Get going," she said. "I'm well rid of you." Her turn to cook, she said. She'd have it waiting for their return. She arranged them both, tugging their collars closer to their throats. "Can't have my men cold. Can't have them going out uncared-for." She giggled. "And watch him, Tom. Don't let Harris hex him, get him running off to sunny Cairo and leaving us alone."

There'd been sun, but all morning clouds had been heading from the Cheviots. Now sleet was falling, making thick splashes on the window of the bus. His father wore brown herringbone coat, brown trilby, brown brogues. Tom kept wiping away the condensation, staring out, watching it form again.

As they entered the city, his father laughed suddenly.

"And skins, all that stuff about skins! He said he'd seen men who'd dress in the skin of a beast and become the beast. Men in leopard skins snarling like leopards. Men wearing antelope skin and leaping high as antelopes. Lion skin, ape skin, snake skin. He reeled them off. Ship's fool. You either ignored him or humoured him. Except the ones that got enough of him, and did their damage in the dark below decks. I found him myself one morning in a heap on the stairs with his clothes all ripped and his skull cracked open. What's happened, I asked him. What've the buggers done? Nothing, he said. Nothing. Harris. Poor sod."

The sleet gathered as slush in doorways and on windowsills. It melted, ran down the gutters towards the quay. The streets were almost deserted, a few people heading down, stooped forward, protecting themselves with umbrellas, wide-brimmed hats, collars tugged tight.

"Can't see him coming out in this," said his father. "We should have stayed. Shouldn't have come."

Tom kept looking up, over the rooftops but the bridge stretched into low-lying clouds, its summit was lost in them. The river was dark grey, agitated by wind and a turning tide. Among the stalls, water dripped from the canopies, the stallholders stared gloomily out.

They ate hot beef sandwiches, and Tom said,

"It's good she didn't come. She'd have hated this."

"Aye. It'd do her no good."

A tinny transistor was playing dance music: a big band, sounding so dated now.

They roamed the alleyways, but found nothing. They halfheartedly inspected the tacky goods for sale. Tom passed over a few coins to buy a brilliant blue scarf for his mother. It was a loosely-woven, inadequate thing, but they praised its colour, said it might be useful when the weather broke. The only place that held them more than a few seconds was the joke stall, where they laughed together at the fake boils and warts, the monkey masks, the turds, the nails that could appear to pierce fingers, the packets of powders and bottles of smells.

Outside, the clouds didn't lift. Beyond the sound of dripping water and music, foghorns wailed from the direction of the sea.

It was useless. He wouldn't come. "Let's go back," said Tom. Relieved, they left the canopies. They were heading back to Dean Street when Tom turned towards the bridge and saw Harris sheltering there. He sat on an upturned crate, the cartwheel was resting at his side, he had a knapsack laid on the ground beside him. Tom took his father's hand, led him there, and Harris kept his face turned towards the earth as they approached. Out of the sleet, beneath the bridge, they relaxed, stood ten yards from Harris.

He wore an ancient and sodden blue striped suit, torn collarless shirt. He had a tweed cap pulled tight over his head. He had a cigarette cupped in his hand, kept drawing on it.

Tom heard his father whispering, "Jesus. Jesus Christ."

Harris tilted his head, was staring back at them. He spat, then held out his hand towards them. Tom felt in his pockets. A few pennies. He went to Harris, dropped them into his palm. He smelt the alcohol on

Harris' breath, saw the scorn in his eyes when he looked down at Tom's offering.

"For this?" he grunted. "For this?"

Tom was backing off but Harris caught him, grabbed his sleeve.

"Him and all," he said. "That bugger there."

Tom's father came forward. He dropped coins of his own into Harris' palm. He stood over him.

"Harris," he said.

Harris stared back at him, empty.

"Do you know me, Harris? Remember me?"

Harris rattled the coins, listening, as if he were enchanted by their ringing.

"We were in Egypt, Harris. We came home on the same boat. You were hurt and I helped to look after you."

Harris stared again.

"You want the wheel?" he said. "The locks and chains? You want to see the needles and the pins stuck in?"

He dropped the coins into his pocket. He made a fist, and stubbed out the cigarette on the back of his hand, laughing as he screwed the cigarette into fragments, leaving the skin black with ash. He wiped it away with his sleeve.

He opened his sack, plunged his hand inside. He took out a packet of safety pins, rolled back his left sleeve, exposing tiny wounds and bruises, a tattoo of a snake wrapped round a bare tree. He began pressing the points into his flesh, pushing until the points emerged again, closing the clasps. When Tom's father recoiled, said, "We don't want that, Harris. We don't want anything," Harris just smiled, sighed. "Just this one," he said. "And this, this..."

"Do you remember Cairo, Harris? The desert? The heat?"

"What now? The locks and chains? Or something new? Something worse, something crueller..? This maybe?" Pulling out from his sack a large fish hook attached to a piece of twine. "Or these?" A hammer, some tweezers, a little saw.

"Nothing, Harris."

Harris' hand reached out again.

"Time to pay again. You and the squirt there. Time to pay."

"We don't want it, Harris.

"Get your loot and pay."

"You remember nothing, Harris?"

Harris stood up now and came at them.

"Think it's over but it's not. Always something else to get through. Always something else to pay for. Get your cash. You, and you and all."

They backed off, out into the sleet again. Beneath the bridge, a small knot of spectators stood watching, sniggering. Harris laughed at them, yelled at them to pay, suddenly reached out, caught Tom's collar.

"The pretty one," he said, and he stared out into the sleet, towards the stalls. "Where's that one? Where's the pretty one?"

Tom recoiled, struggled to free himself.

"Not her and all?" said Harris, and his face contorted as if only now could he feel his pain.

"At home," said Tom. "Couldn't come."

"At home," said Harris and his grip relaxed, Tom pulled away. "Safe at home. Tucked up safe at home."

He went back into the shelter of the bridge, began pulling the pins out from his flesh. He shuddered. "Cold these days," he said, glancing at Tom's father. "So fucking cold." He moved back towards his belongings and crouched there, began assembling his cane and money bag. "But them days," he said. "Them hot days." He stood again, turned round. "And between them days and these days..."

Tom's father caught him by the elbow, stood close to him.

"What?" he asked.

"So hot. So fucking hot. But between them and these..."

And for a moment there was silence, Tom staring at the two men together on the quay, little Harris, ragged and confused, his father bowed over him, moving closer, the two men facing each other as if about to embrace.

"Harris," whispered his father. "What can I do?"

Harris pulled away, with,

"Nothing. Nothing."

And he made his rush at the new spectators, yelling,

"You! I seen you! You been watching and you didn't pay! And you! And you and all..."

They hurried to the station through the sleet. Still early afternoon, but with the clouds so low the streets were darkening. The newspaper-seller was backed deep into a doorway. He flourished a headline at them as they passed. "Get your shelters dug!" he yelled, furious. "Get home and get yourselves prepared!"

"Poor Harris," said his father in the station. "I hardly knew him, just came across him at the end, the journey home. By that time he'd lost everything. Already too far gone."

They leaned close together, watching.

"This one," they said.

"The next one."

"I'll close my eyes. I'll count to ten."

"One and one millionth..."

"Millionths!"

His father pointed to the monument outside.

"See how the angel's getting ready to carry them up? See the dying reaching out to her? See the survivors facing outwards, guns raised, still prepared." Tom peered, screwed up his eyes, distinguished only a heap with the angel silhouetted high above. "Don't believe it, Tom. I saw no angels. What happened to Harris's angel? Where's the angels now, leaning down to help?

Tom leaned closer.

"Will there be another war?"

"What's war? Maybe this is war, still going on. Maybe it's just a longer pause than usual in the fighting. Time to lick the wounds, clean the kit, count the ammo. Maybe when it all starts up again it'll be the same war, the one we thought we'd left behind, and all this time it's just been waiting, biding its time. Maybe there's only ever been one war, all the time getting bigger, nastier. There's them that want it, Tom. There's them can't wait for it."

Their bus arrived, they climbed inside. They were silent, until after the city, out in the dark, among the fields, when Tom went on.

"You said it might just be nothing."

"It might, Tom."

"You said it was just a game."

The man put his arm around the boy, drew him close.

"It is. And maybe we will survive. Maybe we will get through... It's just that between what happened then and what's happening now, between that and this, there was a time when everything seemed possible, when we seemed like children again, a time that really was a kind of heaven..."

And Tom nodded, closed his eyes, saw the calm surface of Derwent Water, the summits of Catbells and Skiddaw shimmering in the summer heat, felt her breath on his cheek, hair on his throat, was surrounded by her scent...

As they approached the village, he opened his eyes. He remained bent over, resting on the coarse damp herringbone, felt the lift of his father's chest, its sighing.

"What's wrong with her?" he said.

"Nothing. Nothing's wrong." The words came too quickly, far too quickly.

"What's wrong with her?"

Long silence, then,

"Nothing, Tom. Nothing."

"Where've you been? Where've my two men been? Just look at you, so brave and cold!"

She fussed at them, unbuttoned their coats for them, kept exclaiming at the cold and damp they'd carried in.

"You shouldn't've gone. Soon as you went I knew you shouldn't, not the way it turned. Awful, awful."

The house was filled with warmth - her cooking all day long, a fire blazing. She drew chairs to the fire for them. She brought them dry socks and trousers, laughed at them as they bumped into each other, changing. They ate from trays balanced on their knees, all of them gathered at the hearth. Her stew with crisp dumplings, buttery carrots, bright spinach. She kept asking about Harris, poor Harris. "Poor soul," said her husband. "I think he's a long way gone." She sighed, clicked her tongue. "We'll have to keep on going to him. We'll give him lots of pennies. We'll try to talk to him, try to get him to see there's other ways, better ways. So sad, Tom? Still cold, I think. Tired and cold." She brought warm cake, poured sauce on it. "Yes?" she asked. "Yes? You can taste the honey in it? So sweet, so warm. Catch every last drop of it, hold it on your tongue a moment more, a moment more. Feel it, Tom, driving out the cold..."

After the food, they kept the television off, the radio off. They sat there in the warmth, listening to the sleet outside and the turning of the sea, their occasional murmurings of content. Tom slept first, and he heard the spectators yelling: Get the chains on! Get the bloody skewer in!

"You're snoring," she said. "Just like you used to years ago." She placed a hot water bottle in his lap, touched his tongue with her finger, a tiny drop of honey on it.

"Upstairs," she told him. "Upstairs, get ready."

She guided him to the door, he heard them laughing as he went up.

The sleet had stopped. The clouds were clearing. Tom left his bed, watched. Moment by moment, more of the Archer was exposed. He stood tall and unmoving over the horizon. How long would it be until the stars dispersed, until the arrow was released? He shuddered. Frost was beginning to form on the window. He closed his eyes, focused deep into the darkness, listened. The sea turned, they gasped and sighed. Was that her cry of pain?

He stared at the stars again, their reflections on the sea.

He imagined bombers, their huge shadows moving across the stars.

He whispered, "When will it begin?"

As he turned to the bed again, the needle pierced his heel. He stifled his cry, squeezed back his tears, lay on his bed and pulled it out. Would her pain be similar to this, would she have to calm it, moment by moment? What would happen when she could not calm it, when there was no peace?

He took the needle, rested its point on his forearm, waited, trembling. Would her fear be similar to this? He pressed, harder, felt the needle breaking through his skin.

"I feel nothing," he whispered. "I'm fine... It's nothing, nothing..."

# Fiesta

The boy can't sleep. The memory of the row, of yet another row, of the father's face aflame, his yelling, "Woman, go to Hell! Go to bloody Hell!"

Now the father sleeps, his snores and grunts and groans fill the dark, and the boy's door opens, his mother comes in with her finger to her lips.

"Come on," she whispers. "Come down."

She hushes him, won't talk to him, won't answer him. She has clothes ready for him downstairs. She helps him dress. She slings a little rucksack on his back. She's grinning as they slip into the night. Away from the house, she urges him onward, grips his hand, drags him, runs through their city, leaving it all behind.

"Where we going?" he keeps asking. "Where will we go?"

No answer, just her soft-soled hurrying feet, her brittle suppressed laughter.

He gives himself up to her, lets himself be led by her. The streets are empty, deserted and dark. The air is icy on his skin. Above the cathedral hangs a huge sickle moon...

Afterwards it will all seem part of a dream: this movement through the city, then the taxi, the airport, the airline desks. He will believe some official carries him aboard: he will retain an image of a beard, a peaked cap, the bitter scent of cigars, bony hands cradling his thighs and back. He will remember that once or twice he wakes, finds himself folded painfully over, head in her lap. He gazes in astonishment up at her. She puts her finger to his lips, sips her whisky, stares out towards the glaring rising sun.

"Just sleep," she whispers. "Just go back to sleep."

Spain. Filthy Bilbao. They stand at the centre on the bridge, look down into the yellow sluggish water. Shit and condoms are floating there. The sun beats down, reducing it like soup, drawing out its stench. A pair of dogs are fighting on the muddy banks. From the factories downstream brown smoke belches into the air.

She takes his hand, leads him over the water in search of Hertz.

She feeds him in a street cafe: huge rolls filled with sweet dried fruit, huge glasses of milky coffee. She drinks shots of cognac and he sees how the red begins to bruise the whites of her eyes.

He watches a rat scuttle from a drain grid, slip into a butcher's doorway. He says nothing, pushes his plate away. He's stopped asking her questions now, he wants only to lie in a soft dark place and sleep again.

"We'll move on again," she tells him. "It's no distance to the sea."

He holds his arms up, protection from the sun. Already his skin is burning.

She finds Hertz, drives them away in a little white Seat down towards the sea.

Castro Urdiales: little stone harbour and huge stone church and long white beaches where tourists lie waiting for fiesta to begin. In the town square a stage is set with amplifiers and microphones, bunting and fairy lights are tangled in the trees. She finds them a hostale close by, El Cordobes, room with wrought iron balcony looking out to the square and then the sea. She sits hugging him on his bed, gradually lowers him until he is prone and sleeping. She leaves him there, walks out to learn the place. When he wakes the sun is falling, he is alone, he listens for his father's snores, his breath gulps in his throat. He stares out from the balcony. Above the harbour walls a high wire has been erected, straddling the water, stretched between two cranes. Tables are arranged on the quays, barbecues are burning, somewhere someone rehearses with a bass guitar, a dull and simple sequence repeated and repeated. Children in Sunday frocks and suits climb among the staging, watched by laughing parents and grandparents. On the crowded pavement directly below he sees her, head propped on her hand, bottle of wine at her elbow, at a table filled with togged-up performers - men with lacquered hair, white body suits, red bandannas.

He goes down, ruffled, bleary-eyed, steps shyly from the door into the tangle of bodies and babble of voices, can't see through to her till she's calling him, "Here, darling! Here I am!"

He stands squeezed between her and the blondest of the men, who has nothing but a thin-strapped singlet covering his chest, exposing a tangle of hair, thick arm muscles, letting out the sourness of his sweat.

"Luciano," she says.

"Luciano," says the man. He takes the boy's hand, squeezes it tight. He points to the wire above the quays. "Luciano. Artista of the sky."

She lets him sip her wine but it quenches nothing. He asks for water and she nods, goes on listening to the men. They talk in their own impenetrable tongue, but Luciano keeps turning to her, trying to involve her.

"Tonight," he says, and he winks at the boy, flexes his arm muscles. "You will see of what we are made tonight."

Out in the square two jugglers toss spinning knives towards each other. A thin man on stilts wearing women's clothes bends down and tickles children. Past the church tower the sun sinks blazing into the sea. The fairy lights come on, a brass band starts playing, Luciano leans across and kisses her hand.

"From below you will watch us, I think," he says. "From the tables."

He goes away into the crowd with his friends.

The boy asks for water. She gives him more wine. She points into the square, to the children playing.

"Go and enjoy yourself," she says.

He stares out into the crowds.

"Go on," she says.

He goes out. Children run past him, bump into him, ignore him. The man on stilts stretches down and tickles him. Suddenly at his side there is a whoosh of fire and black plume of smoke stretching to the sky. A stench of kerosene, English voices:

"Burned me bastard hair again."

Three of them, in jeans and stained T shirts, little dirty bottles in their hands. The fat one takes a sip, balloons his cheeks, leans his head back, holds a lighted torch before his lips, breathes another stream of flame into the air. A few children watch. A little applause from the adults. The three of them stand in triangular formation with torches by their faces, breathe a pyramid of fire stretching high above their heads. Then they walk out into the square, cardboard boxes in their hands, asking in sign language for coins. They call to each other, laugh at each other. They'll get enough to get pissed on then start again. He picks up their names: Lasky and Squealer and Ken. Squealer's breath close by is rich in kerosene, his hair is singed to nothing at his brow.

"I've got nothing," says the boy.

"An Englishman! A civilised being." He stretches out his arms in mock thanksgiving. "And when did you come down?"

But his mother is at his side, taking his hand, moving him on, followed by Squealer's wolf-whistles and smacking lips.

They sit at a table below the searchlit wire. She buys grilled sardines and salad and bread to be eaten with forks and fingers. Scales and soot stick to the skin, oil drips from the leaves. The boy wipes himself with bread while his mother gasps and Luciano steps out into almost-nothingness high above. He stands up, moves between the tables towards the braziers. He makes drinking motions to the chef, who holds up wine and beer to him.

"Water," the boy says, and the chef scoffs, points to the sea, holds his hands out to the sky.

"Luciano!" he calls. "Luciano, olé!"

Later, Luciano comes to them, alone this time. He holds her hand.

"At the most dangerous of movements, you it was I thought of," he says.

They sit close. They watch the boy.

"So tired, my little one?" she asks.

"No," he tells her, but she just laughs, so indulgent.

He notices how she sways in walking, how she holds Luciano's muscular arm so tight. The celebrations continue. Fire and smoke belch into the air, the children play, the stiltwalker claps in tune with a singer on the stage. She takes him to the room, helps him from his clothes, tucks him in his bed. She strokes his brow, so loving.

"Sleep," she whispers, then goes back down to Luciano.

He doesn't sleep. Thirst, heat, the noise outside. She doesn't return. Deep into the night, fireworks explode, a rock band begins to roar. He goes downstairs in his vest, finds the entry thronged with folk. In the bar there is a tap, a little washbasin. He goes to it, holds his head down, gulps the water, soaks himself with water.

Next morning, she's shaking him awake. Sunlight streams in at the window. There are drummers drumming outside. She claps her hands for him.

"Aren't we so lucky to have arrived at a fiesta!"

They go exploring, head through green valleys and wooded foothills to the mountains. Soon great sheer walls of craggy rock are glaring before them in the sun. The nearer they approach, the more the heat and light intensify. They keep passing solitary walkers with rucksacks and boots and wooden staffs and bulbous water carriers at their waists.

"Who are they?" she says. "Who the hell are they?"

In the afternoon they halt at Fuente De, where a pair of cable cars travel steeply up onto the distant rock. They buy tickets, lounge with hundreds of others in a green park, waiting for their number to be called. They watch the cars rising and falling, see hordes of tourists bussed in. Many are turned away: too late, so many waiting. A few pick their way hopefully through the crowd, seeking to buy a place. The boy's skin is red and scorched now. She buys cream, gently rubs it into him, saying he'll soon get used to this.

She closes her eyes going up. He stands gripping the rail, stares through the glass towards the diminishing park. The car is smooth and swift at first, but it slows and trembles, hauled through the final almost-perpendicular reaches of the cable.

At the top are a souvenir shop and drinks stall, a steel platform slung across the drop, families on benches pointing out across the foothills to the sea. Many are taking photographs, others grip the earth, pretending that at any minute they could fall. Behind all this, stony footpaths climb higher towards sharp and far-off summits. Nothing of green, just rock and scree and fallen boulders, everything bleached and baked by the sun. They begin to walk. Others walk before them, several with tents and sleeping-rolls on their backs. At each ridge, the nearest peaks, those he'd imagined they'd reach, appear to retreat. The others walk on, seeming unconcerned. "Where can they hope to get to?" she asks. She calls out to one as he passes: an older man, in boots and shorts, massive sack standing high above his shoulders. "Where do you hope to go?" But he understands nothing, just shrugs, grins, plods on his way. The boy asks to go on, but they rest on stones and she sighs and talks of her thumping heart, the effects of last night's wine. The boy begins to scream, waiting for echoes from the cliff before screaming again. Then come other voices, more subdued but also echoing through silence, and they discern brilliantly-clothed rock climbers far above. And then are birds, surely eagles, wheeling slowly in the luminous and empty air.

They go back down. The boy keeps finding crevices where snow lies frozen, hard and dry as the rock itself. He keeps plunging his hand in, gasping at the cold, leaning down to lick. She scolds him and urges him onward: the sun is falling, the cars will stop, fiesta will begin. They continue in silence, stepping aside to let through those with heavy loads.

At the brink, shielding their eyes, they gaze out: the cable cars and village, the foothills, the coastal plain, white towns, blue stripe of sea. To the west, more mountains, green and sombre below unmoving clouds. He turns, rests his eyes there.

"Come on," she tells him. "Wake up. Come on."

The dropping of the car feels uncontrolled. She closes her eyes, holds her breath, grips him tight. He watches the earth speeding at them. He prepares to announce their coming death, but they brake, decelerate, shudder back into place.

Out on the road again, parallel with the sea, they begin to see again those walkers with staffs and bulbous water carriers.

She slows down, pulls up by one of them, winds her window down.

"Who are you?" she begs.

"Pilgrims." A gentle smile. The man holds up a medal of Saint James. He shows the scallop shell embroidered on his shirt. "We take the ancient way to Santiago. It reduces time in Purgatory. It is a journey for the sake of God." He leans forward, looks in at the boy and winks at him. He presses upon him a postcard of the city, its streets glistening with water. "It is El Orinal de Espana. The pisspot. It rains and rains. But you must go one day, ease your way to Heaven."

She drives away ferociously, muttering of holy fools, evil ideas sewn in the simple minds of children. She grabs the postcard, flings it from the window.

"Heaven! Bloody Heaven!"

It is almost dark in Castro Urdiales. Many cars and many walkers entering. The noise of bands and drummers travels to the outskirts, intensifies as they go further in. At the centre, above the heads, the plumes of smoke and flame, the stiltwalkers, the spotlit wire. They pause at Hostale El Cordobes, just long enough for her to wipe him clean, to change into a thin dark dress and peer into his eyes.

"All right, my love? Ready to fiesta?"

Below the wire Luciano is waiting for them. He asks about their day, he hugs the boy, he orders wine for them. Then he sits next to her with his arm around her and they turn to face the darkness out at sea. They whisper together, intense, hardly-comprehensible. There are mutterings of early days, of pride, of falling.

"Those days now are gone," he says. "At last we are free." He kisses them, takes his leave. "The sky it awaits. I will return to you."

They have sardines again, and bread and salad and wine. Smoke from the braziers keeps drifting over the tables. As they eat, Luciano steps out, and the crowd applauds, roars.

"Luciano!" they call. "El Artista Luciano! Luciano olé!"

She gazes upward, open-mouthed, hands spread in fright across her cheeks. The boy nibbles at the fish, imagining Santiago with its peaceful pilgrims and its rain. He wipes his hands with bread, swigs wine from her glass. When Luciano has crossed the wire, she makes fists of joy, reaches out to hold the boy.

"Will we go to Santiago?" he asks.

"Santiago!" she scoffs. She is irritated by the word. She points upward to the sky. "We have fiesta, we have Luciano! Enjoy yourself. Who needs God and drizzle?"

And she gasps again, as Luciano steps out again.

He says he is going to the square to find other children to play with.

"Good," she tells him, shifting her gaze from the sky to him and back again. "Play like they do! Enjoy fiesta!" She thrusts some coins at him. "Don't worry! We'll each know where the other is."

He walks away from the excited cries, the upturned faces, he twists through the crowd.

In the square, children climb on the staging. An ancient woman turns a rope for skipping girls, and chants skipping songs with them. A lacklustre band tunes guitars. The fire-eaters sprawl ignored beneath a statue, giggling and cursing and holding dark bottles to their lips.

"Castro Urdiales," Squealer yells. "Castro Bloody Urdiales! Arsehole of the world!"

The boy sits on a bench, faces the harbour, watches spotlit distant Luciano, and prays that he will fall. He doesn't fall. The performance ends, the crowd beneath the wire disperses, the square becomes more populous again. The stiltwalker taps him on the shoulder, makes a sad face then a happy face, and tickles him, inviting imitation of his smile. The boy moves away. Then he sees her, with Luciano, coming towards the square. He sees how she keeps glancing from side to side, as if searching for him, but wary of finding him. She grips Luciano tight. The boy backs into the crowds, watches them cross the square and enter El Cordobes.

Warily, he follows. He scans the tables outside, he scans the inside bar. He licks his lips. He goes to the tap and gulps the water. At the foot of the stairs he hesitates, then he climbs, stands stockstill on the landing, at their door.

From inside, his mother: "Luciano! Oh artista Luciano!"

He stands for minutes, listening. He attempts to remember his father. He thinks of cool damp streets, the comforting touch of pilgrims.

"Luciano!" she calls. "Luciano, olé!"

Outside again, he stands before the fire-eaters.

"I smell an Englishman!" yells Squealer. "But where's the pretty Englishwoman?"

He kneels by the boy. He waits for the boy to drop a coin into the box. He sips at the kerosene, leans back, balloons his cheeks, sends a thin jet of liquid into the air, touches it with the torch and it bursts with a thump into flame.

He laughs, hisses air between his teeth, dribbles kerosene and saliva.

"Fire-eating," he whispers. "How'd you like a go?"

The boy just stares.

"It's easy. Dead easy."

Squealer opens his mouth wide.

"Put your tongue like this so none gets to your throat. Then your lips, just like you're kissing. Then you blow it out, nice and thin and smooth. Watch."

He sips from the tiny bottle, he blows out the thin smooth stream. He raises the torch, the liquid bursts to flame.

"Try it," he says. "No fire this time. Just the kerosene and the blowing out."

He raises the bottle to the boy's lips.

"A sip," he whispers. "Just a little sip."

The boy sips. He cannot control his mouth. He gags, swallows and retches. He stares wildly back at Squealer and Squealer roars with laughter.

"Not like that! Not like bloody that! Like I showed you." Then his voice lowers again. "It's OK. We're all the same at first but we learn to take it. Try again, boy. Take another sip."

The boy is going to be sick. He can feel it. Squealer comforts him.

"Just a matter of practice," he whispers.

He shows it again: how to shape the mouth, how to blow it out, how to light. Fire and smoke thump into the air. The boy recoils. He sees Lasky and Ken arrive at Squealer's side.

"Getting another one started," says Squealer. He raises the bottle to the boy's lips again. "Take another sip," he says.

"Go on," says Lasky.

"Fucking go on, lad," says Ken. "Take another sip."

Squealer presses the bottle harder to his lips. "Anyway," he whispers, "Where's the sexy mother?"

The boy retches again.

They crouch down with him. Lasky puts his arms around him, holds him there.

"We'll make a fire-eater of you yet," says Ken.

"Where is she?" whispers Squealer.

The boy twists his head to El Cordobes, sees the tightly-fastened shutters at their window. He feels the coarse hands and fierce breath of the fire-eaters. His mouth is burning. He is in despair. He knows that he will never return to his father, that he will never get to Santiago, never feel its gentle rain. He abandons himself to them, prepares to sip again.

"She's with Luciano," he says. "Luciano, artist of the sky."

# Lucy Blue

I'd not seen Lucy Blue for years, and then the parcel came: the key to her house, the sharpened knife, the scribbled note: Key will let you in. Knife will end it. Please come to me. Set me free.

Lucy Blue. We were children together. We were little girls with skirts tucked into our knickers splashing in the surf. She lived with her mother in a timber house way out on the headland. Beside them was the lighthouse whose light brilliantly swept the world at night. Beyond them was the cold Northumbrian sea, its chain of islands stretching to the horizon.

Her father was far away, and had been since she was born. She said he was a pirate chief swashbuckling his way across the hot seas of the south. When he sailed back he'd be laden with jewels and exotic fruits for us, he'd bring monkeys to play in the dunes and parrots to whistle in the pines. He'd take us away beyond the islands in his gorgeous sailing ship.

Sometimes as the dusk gathered and the lighthouse light began to spin, as I prepared to make my way back along the shore to my dull village, she'd grip me tight:

If you love me you'll believe me. It will be like that. You'll see.

She waited and the years passed. Her mother painted the house as white as the lighthouse. She had cables laid from the village and switches and power points and dangling bulbs installed in every room. She laughed with Lucy:

We'll make sure he won't miss us when he comes sailing in!

And then at last he came, and we saw, and Lucy and I were children no longer. He was ragged and hunched, his face was blackened with stubble and rage. There was cider in his pockets and slurred curses on his tongue. He reeled from his wife and drooled and smacked his lips for the pretty little thing he'd spawned.

And when I felt his gaze fall upon me I scurried homeward through the dunes.

In the village, there were rumours of drug smuggling, and jail sentences in distant places. The people turned their backs to him. One day in The Angel there was a knife fight and one of the village hard boys was cut from cheek to chin. When they came to the headland at dusk to wreak revenge, the man's venom as he ran at them sent them fleeing as if from Hell.

I was forbidden to go there. At night I peered from my window. I watched the miles-long wedge of light sweeping the sea, the land, the sea again. As it passed, I squeezed my eyes against its glare. I tried to discern the glow of Lucy's house above the dunes. I prayed. I cried for her. I whispered to her, as if there were another cable linking her life to mine

Lucy, I think of you still. Lucy, I love you still.

But more time passed, I felt myself growing away from her, my mind was drawn by other things.

And then we learned of the fate of her mother. She was lifted in a trawl net with her skull broken and with stones packed into the lining of her winter coat. Two detectives from Tyneside came to the village, went out to Lucy's place, returned without her father. They took lunch in The Angel and shrugged at all the questions. There was nothing on the man, they murmured. And they drove away.

After the funeral I went out there again. Lucy wore white like a bride and she told me that her mother had not really gone. She told me to stay until dark and see. All afternoon, I held her hand at the table.

Lucy, I whispered. Come back with me!

From deeper in the house came the muttering and cursing of her father, his snores, his whimperings, his calling from the depths of awful dreams. He lurched into the doorway at dusk, grunting some praise of the pretty little girls of Bangkok and Ceylon.

Lucy, I whispered. Come back with me!

He staggered closer. I saw the knife shoved down inside his belt. I smelt his livid breath. His eyes reeled and his tongue rolled on his lips as he reached for me.

I ran home weeping through the swinging floods of light.

When I next went back I found her sitting on the shore. All around her were scattered switches and power points and bulbs. Electric cables and wire were tangled in the heaped-up weed. She laughed and told me it was better this way. He'd ripped out everything. He'd said he couldn't bear to have light getting everywhere, exposing everything. She giggled, and held me, and drew me to the house. He was wrong, she said. It's the light that blocks out everything. If I came inside and waited until dark, I'd truly see.

Inside were the scents of candles and burned paraffin. Again his whisperings and cries from further in. I held my friend, I gazed into her eyes.

Lucy, I whispered. Come back with me.

She smiled. We waited. I wept for the life that was being drained from her and she stroked my hand in order to comfort me.

Soon the lighthouse light began its pulse: long periods of dark and sudden bursts of light. I must just relax, she said. I must gaze about me in the room. I must allow myself to see. Outside, the darkness deepened. I imagined the long stretch of shore between me and my home. I trembled and she soothed me: it was all right, everything was all right. Wait until the light had passed and focus on the dark. The dark, each time a little darker. Soon I'd see.

There! she gasped. There!

She gripped me, nails biting my flesh.

There! You have to see her! There!

I stared across the table. The white flare of Lucy's face and dress plunged in and out of dark. Her eyes swivelled, she glared through me and past me and at me.

Oh, see! she begged me. Please see!

I heard him coming through the house.

Lucy! Please come back with me!

The door swung open and I ran.

And didn't stop running until I'd made a future for myself that was nothing to do with this place, and nothing to do with my friend.

And then, as if they had pursued me ever since that night: the key, the knife, the note: Key will let you in. Knife will end it. Please...

It was a day-long journey. I drove to the village, the dull place. I parked outside The Angel. I trudged through the dunes to the shore. The falling sun lit up the house and lighthouse way out on the headland. All along the beach were stinking heaps of weed and stranded jellyfish, the endless line of waste thrown up by the sea. The sea itself was hardly moving, it was oily and flat, lazily slopping against itself where it met the shore. Not a soul to be seen. Closer to, I saw how Lucy's mother's paint had begun to peel away, how the timbers had distorted and cracked. Doors and windows were tight shut. I thought of calling but the words just gurgled in my throat. There were footprints in the sand, but leading everywhere, no way of learning anything from them.

I reached for the door and my heart began to thunder and the world grew dark. Locked. I whimpered, taking the key, inserting it, turning it. Shuddering as I did, I nicked my skin, caused drops of blood on the key, the door, the handle.

Oh, Lucy! I prayed. Just come outside. Come back with me.

I turned the handle and went inside. The table as always. The candle and paraffin scents. The scent of the man: alcohol, bitterness and sweat. I stood in a corner of the room beside the door. The name I would cry still gurgled uselessly in my throat. From outside came the final screaming of the gulls as the light began to turn.

Lucy! I whispered. Where are you, Lucy?

But nothing, just time plunging onwards, intensifying the darkness, intensifying the light. I felt my tears running, heard the draughts in the timbers, the turning sea, something shuffling somewhere on the sand. I steeled myself, I gripped the handle of the knife, I stared into the dark, each time a little darker.

Lucy! Where are you, Lucy? I've come to see you, Lucy..

And then there she was, so sudden and so clear, in the opposite dark corner - the white bloom of her bridal dress, her smiling eyes in the white bloom of her face.

Oh, Lucy! I gasped, and I reached towards her. Come back with me, Lucy!

She disappeared in the pulse of light, reappeared in the stretch of dark.

Her lips opened and closed as if to welcome me but no sound came.

What is it, Lucy?

She drew back the collar of her dress, showed me the bruises and the lacerations, and then she smiled again, so joyous, and I began to see beside her the other woman, more obscure in her dark winter coat, and my heart leapt, and I said.

Oh, Lucy! I see! I truly see!

I moved towards them, but as I moved the light turned once more and showed me the man approaching on the beach.

I stepped back into the dark behind the door. I smiled across at my friend. I raised the sharpened knife. I waited for him to enter, this false pirate chief, this father, this fiend...

# Instead of the Scheme

All that week, the weather didn't change. On Friday Mickey just stood there on the doorstep in his shorts, with his overalls slung over his back. I knew he was going to say it again.

"Sod the scheme. Let's go to the beach instead."

All that week I'd told him no, but this time I shrugged and told him to hang on. I went back in, changed into my trunks, heard my mother coming up after me.

"Come on Rob," she shouted. "Don't slip back. Don't waste your good work now."

I pulled my overalls back on, had to push past her on the stairs.

"Get out there," she said. "Move. And get those buttons fastened up."

We laughed about her as we headed for the Metro, cutting through the back streets to keep out of sight. At Heaton Road we rested and looked through the traffic at the other lads lined up outside the church waiting for Norman to arrive.

"See?" said Mickey. "See how bloody tame they are?"

I pulled him back into the lanes.

"Bloody right," I told him. "Come on, run. You've got to do it, got to break loose sometime."

We kept going as far as Byker, where all the terraces had gone, where you could see right out over the city to the bridges and the river and the hills twenty miles away. For once the whole place seemed shining and still, nothing but a gentle roar coming out of it. I held him back, told him to take it in. I wanted to tell him how foreign it was, how different it could be. But we had to run again when we saw the yellow Metro swerving out from underground and coming up the hill.

The Metro was packed. It was the holidays. There were hundreds of children on with their parents. I was shoved into the aisle, but Mickey stayed by the door with space all around him. I saw how people watched him, how they couldn't take their eyes off him, how he just stood there dead calm, as if nothing could ever bother him. "He's a proud one," my mother had always said, and it was true. I'd know that from the first time I ever saw him, last year at the start of the scheme. Norman had taken us round the church, told us all the changes that had to be made. He took me aside and whispered, "Any objection to pairing up with the laddo there?" I looked at the others laid out on the altar steps, passing round the fags, then back at Mickey all alone with the light from the stained glass windows pouring down at him. I shrugged and said he looked all right. "Good lad," said Norman. "I could see you're one with sense." Then he grinned. "Don't let him hex you, mind."

Most people were set to stay on to the coast, but at Wallsend a few men shuffled off for the yards. I squeezed onto a seat beside a man with a huge carrier on his knee, stuffed with towels and food and bottles of home brew. His kids were piled up at the window, staring out. He wanted to talk. He asked where I was working, but when I started to tell him, his little girl started crying and he had to concentrate on calming her down. I laughed with him and just sat back, enjoying rattling along past the cranes on the river, reading the spray on the walls of the old factories - lots of faded writing about the NF and aggro, then the new stuff that started in America or somewhere, beautifully-painted cartoons, massive patterns of monsters and heros, things that must have taken nights and nights to make.

At Tynemouth, walking down towards the Priory, Mickey burst out laughing at me. He tugged my overalls open and held his hand on his eyes as if I dazzled him. Get them off, he told me. I couldn't go onto a beach like that. I was on the loose. Free. He put his hand inside, started to roll the overalls off my shoulders.

"Howay, Rob. Where's your style?"

I felt ridiculous, standing there on the pavement, stripping down to my trunks and trainers. But I had to laugh, and once we were walking again I did start to feel freer, more like him. I told him it was like the dream where you're caught in town with nothing on, and he said aye, he knew that one all right.

We leaned on the blue railings at the bottom of the street. The long beach that stretched north was still deserted, but underneath the Priory dozens of people were already laid out on towels and children were splashing in the water. Everybody knew this was the best beach. With the cliffs all around and the tide going out, it would be like an oven by twelve-o-clock.

We ran down the steps to it. There wasn't a breath of wind down there, and the sea was gentle, just going sh sh as it went out. A smell of coffee and bacon came from the tiny cafe against the cliffs, and closer to the sea we caught the sweet smell of suntan lotion from the girls. We left our things in a heap, ran, dived, and came up hooting at the cold. But you always get used to it, and soon we were swimming across the bay, me practising my strokes, trying to move like I'd been taught at school, so smooth that I hardly made a splash, and Mickey disappearing again and again when he dived to touch the floor. He started to come up under me, pulling me down to the icy cold and dark, where we wrestled in the seaweed before bursting up to the top again. I was worn out when I finally kicked free of him and swam back to the sand. He came out ages later, dripping wet and sparking with the sun behind him, his hands full of tiny shells that he scattered all over me.

We spread out our overalls and lay on them. I kept talking about the church, about what the others would be doing now, trapped in there while we were here. I said,

"Sometimes you want it to be like this. Like nothing else. It lets you see things properly when it's like this." I used the words I'd heard so many times from him. "You see how they try to make you something you don't want to be."

He said nothing.

"Don't you?" I said.

He leaned up, shading his eyes from the sun, and looked at me.

"Aye," he said. "They get you slowly, bit by bit."

Then he lay quiet again with his eyes closed, letting the sun beat down on him. He kept stretching, digging his toes and his fingers into the sand. I watched the white salt showing on his skin as he dried. I watched the tattoo that filled his back. The red eyes were coloured in, and the red tongue, and the black inside its mouth. Different scales were different colours, all the others were his own smooth brown. Lying there beside him in the heat, I could hardly stop myself from tracing the outline, feeling the empty scales and the coloured scales, searching his skin with my spread fingers. "Mickey," I whispered after a while, wanting to talk to him and get to know him, but he didn't move and he didn't speak.

I knew them well, these times he went so far into himself it seemed I'd never get him back. They made me understand the other lads, how they'd ask, "Why do you want to hang about with him? What is he? Nowt but a ponced-up coon with a fancy tongue and a big tattoo. Get rid of him." Sometimes I thought all that myself, especially on Friday nights when I went down into town with them. "Where's the coon?" they'd ask, after a few drinks. "How's the chocolate licking?" But I didn't care. It was great after a week of work to be out there in the crowd, going from bar to bar, looking for girls to take into shop doorways or under bridges. Nights like that, Mickey seemed a world away as if there was, like they said, something twisted in him. It used to worry my mother at first, me coming home drunk in the middle of the night, but my dad understood. He told her to stop fussing. I had to learn. I had to find my way. Saturday mornings I spent flat out in bed with my head throbbing, thinking back to the time we'd had. I hated it when Mickey came looking for me then. My mother wouldn't let him come upstairs, so I'd go down and stand there on the doorstep with him. "Out with the lads again, eh?" he'd say. "Aye, that's the style." I knew then why the others wanted nothing to do with him, why they used to say, "He'll get what's coming, mind. Watch out you're not around."

The tattoo had been coming for months, since just after the scheme started. It was a snake with its tail inside his shorts, its coils all the way up his back, its head high and its mouth open wide at his neck. Every Thursday he went after work to get five pounds worth of it coloured in. The first time we saw it was in April, when the weather started to change. We were in the graveyard with our lunchboxes when he rolled down his overalls. Norman burst out laughing. He'd seen it all, he said. Now he'd seen it all. And how much was that costing, son? Mickey stared at him, then he told him. Norman went on laughing, but I could see the other lads didn't know what to think. They kept looking at the ground, then at each other, like they were waiting for something. It just took one of them to start, and soon they were all giggling like a pack of kids. I tried to catch Mickey's eye, to let him know I wasn't in with them, but he took no notice.

He just shook his head and lay down on the grass between the graves, sunbathing. That afternoon Norman told Mickey he was going too far. He was making things worse for himself. Nobody would ever take him on if they got a glimpse of it. Maybe there was a way of getting rid of it. But Mickey laughed right in Norman's face, and boasted about the tiger he'd planned for his chest. When I said Norman might be worth listening to, he bared his teeth at me and said nothing else all day.

All morning they kept streaming down the steps, so many of them you wondered how the beach would ever take them all. But it did take them, with their umbrellas and air beds and plastic chairs, and we still kept our thin circle of empty sand around us. By lunchtime, it was as if there was some huge party going on. Music was blaring out from radios. Kids kept running past, screaming and kicking up the sand. Outside the cafe two men in sawn-off jeans sat on tall red chairs looking out to sea. They had loudhailers for when anything went wrong, but they just used them for shouting and singing to the crowd. Every few minutes it was Hi de Hi, getting everybody to yell back their Ho de Ho. The air was filled with the smell of food. Packets and boxes were being opened. White cartons and wooden forks were being carried from the cafe. I opened my own box and tapped Mickey's shoulder. "Dinner break," I told him, repeating Norman's daily joke, "Time to hit the tombs," but he took an age to come round then wanted nothing but to share my orange and get the sea out of his mouth. He peered at the people, amazed to see them all. He cursed at the noise, but he laughed, saying how easy it was to make them pleased, and didn't mean it like he sometimes did.

"I mean, look," he said, pointing at the man I'd sat with on the Metro. His kids had dug a hole for him, and he was stretched out in it, grinning as they used their little spades to bury him.

"It's all they need, Rob, isn't it? Nothing much, just this."

"Yes. Good weather. Simple pleasures."

"Aye. Ha!" He grinned as he picked a pip from his teeth. "But what the hell, eh? It's just to keep you down. You're allowed a little bit of this, but it's just to keep you down."

I agreed again, and I started to say something about finding a way of never having to work. But I kept it back. We'd said it all before, and anyway I knew it was different for me than it would ever be for Mickey. I might have broken out today, but I knew I'd learned from the scheme about how places are made and how to fix them. I knew the scheme might work for me and I might somehow get a job through it. I wanted to work. I wanted to get my own place someday and make it fine. But what did

Mickey want? Sometimes he seemed so clever you'd think he could do anything. Even Norman said it was Mickey who had the quickest head and the quickest hands. Once I'd watch him strip a stained glass window to its separate parts, clean it up, then reassemble it perfectly. It was wonderful, real craftsman's work. None of the rest of us would have even known where to start. But when I told him that, he just laughed and started to prise out pieces of the glass and sent them skidding across the floor into the rubble. "Better like that, eh?" he said, looking down at some saint outside a city with little holes all around him. Later he leaned against the wall and watched me hunting for the pieces then forcing them back into place. I was so clumsy I botched the whole thing, twisted the frame, tearing the lead, so it looked hardly any better than when he'd started. That was the first time I swore at him. "You sod, Mickey. You fucking sod." But of course he just went on grinning and called me poor lad. I could have strangled him. I saw that even about him and me I didn't know. We'd had nearly a year of working together, but once the year was over and the scheme was done with, there was no way of knowing if I'd ever see him again.

He was watching a girl wading onto the beach. She was tall and thin and her wet hair was clinging to her shoulders. She had a silver chain around her waist and her costume had metal threads in it, making it shine like gold. At the water's edge she sat facing the sea with the water rising and falling across her legs. I watched her with him. She was so beautiful, nearly as brown as he was, as if she'd spent months in another warmer place. And I watched him. I'd not seen him with girls before. He hardly taked about them, not like the other lads about who he'd had and who he wanted, but I could tell by the way he looked that he wanted her.

It didn't bother him. He just stood up, told me to watch his things, walked down to her. My heart was racing. I was sure she'd send him away. Maybe it was because he did it all without any fuss that she let him sit with her. They talked easily, and were soon making each other laugh. Once she turned, gave me a sudden smile, a wave and I found myself willing her to stay with him, love him. I lay back. Already I could feel my skin beginning to burn. The sun was glaring from above the ruins of the priory and I couldn't look at the sky. I tried to imagine finding a girl for myself, the four of us spending the whole summer together on the beach, getting brown, being free, needing nothing. I tried to lie quiet and still like Mickey had. I heard all the noise dying as if the heat had stunned everyone. Somewhere a woman screeched at her children to shut up, to settle down. I couldn't stand it. I sat forward again, just in time to see

Mickey and the girl enter the sea. They were wonderful, Mickey with his bright tattoo and his shorts flapping at his legs, the girl with her tiny gold bikini and the skin between her bottom and her legs creasing and uncreasing as she walked forward. They swam out slowly in a dead straight line from the centre of the beach, then turned towards the rocky headland below the priory. Out there the water was like glass. They moved with long smooth strokes, their heads dipping into and out of the water, until they disappeared behind the rocks, and all you could see was their wake.

There was no shade. The few caves in the cliffs already had families in them, squatting around baskets of food and steaming jugs. I waited for a while, but I had to leave. I took my money and my trainers and picked my way over the bodies towards the steps. I climbed slowly, kept stopping to scan the water, but caught no sign of them. At the top a cool breeze was blowing off the land. Outside The Gibraltar Rock men on holiday or on the dole leaned against the walls drinking beer. They wore light clothes with their shirts open wide, and their wives and children sat by them on white chairs beneath umbrellas. Walking past them all towards the door, I knew that if only it could be summer always, the place might still not be grand or rich, but it might be fine, with no problems for anyone.

I drank in the cellar bar, enjoying the moist half-darkness after the hot beach. The first drink hardly touched the sides. I sipped the second, glancing into the mirror behind the bar, smiling at how red my face and shoulders were, but thinking that this might be the beginning of my first real tan. When I went out again I looked and saw the overalls spread out on the sand with nobody near them. I climbed the grassy slope to the priory gates. The notices said that the north had been born in these ancient places. By the time the Vikings came to destroy the buildings, murder the monks and rape the nuns, it was too late to put a stop to everything. From the gates I could see where the river met the sea. On the opposite bank girders were screeching and thumping onto concrete as the warehouses were ripped down. Further in, the cranes were dead still, waiting their turn. Beyond them, I saw nearly as far as Newcastle. I tried to imagine the river and everything I saw with all the workplaces gone. I tried to imagine the past, before Tynemouth, before Newcastle, before any of this, when there were just rough fields and woods along the backs, the roads just dirt and the towns little rings of smoking huts. I tried to see everything lifted away, to see what was underneath it all, like when we had torn out the floor of the church and Norman had said we were looking at ground that hadn't been seen for centuries. But it was too much to deal with. It was easier to look at maps and see all the little crosses spreading out from Tynemouth, Durham, Lindisfarne, taking the whole place over, making it change. I could see it like a pattern then, but I still couldn't take it in, not really.

With no one watching the gate I slipped inside without paying. I expected to see everything laid out, labels everywhere, exhibits displayed in glass cases. I expected to see what our church would be, but on a grander scale. But behind the huge front wall there were just broken archways and bits of stone column and trenches to show where the walls had been. The slopes down to the cliffs were packed with graves worn almost smooth by wind and spray. I saw how perfect it must have seemed here, to have the protection of so many cliffs and so much water, and I saw why they'd chosen this place for the newer buildings at the point - the coastguard station, the low concrete gun emplacement left over from the war. I went right out there and stood above where the guns had been. Behind me, for miles on either side, the shores were crammed. In front, everything was empty, shining, motionless. My whole body was trembling. I felt exposed, all alone, as if I had truly broken free of the scheme and my parents, and I began to tell myself, This is where you start to change and grow. Then my head began to reel and I had to crouch on all fours, collecting myself. That was when I saw them, far below on a tiny stretch of sand. They lay side by side with their few clothes scattered around them. I waved and waved, but they must have been sleeping or keeping out of the glare. I lay for minutes across the concrete waiting for them to wake and move, then I saw that the shadow of the headland would soon reach them. Soon they would go back to the beach. I turned towards the gates again. Walking into the sun, I had to hold the gravestones as I tottered through, knowing that at any moment I could collapse.

Half the beach was in shadow. The sunbathers had shifted closer to the sea. Families were gathering their belongings, coming past me on the steps as I went heavily down, gripping the handrail for support. At the foot I dropped to the sand, leaned on the rock. I must have fallen asleep. I found the little girl in front of me, holding out the overalls.

"Mister. Mister. Dad said give you these, Mister."

Behind her, the man I'd met that morning waved at me, then he turned and yelled at the water, telling his other children to get out.

"Thank you," I said, taking the overalls, beginning to pull mine on. My teeth were chattering. I was icy cold.

"Not that they'd've got nicked," he said when he came to us with his packed carrier. "Tide'd've got them, though. Look at the little sods. They'll do owt but what they're told." He looked down at me. I was struggling to fasten the buttons at my throat. And he grinned like my father would, half-amused, half-concerned.

"Been drinking then?" he asked.

"Hardly anything."

"It doesn't help, though, does it?"

I shook my head.

"You're not used to this, are you? This weather?"

"No."

"Thought not. I watched you all morning, you and your mate. He'll be bad, I thought. He'll be suffering tonight. Here." He passed me a half-full bottle of lemonade. "It's what you need. You're all dried out."

I drained the bottle, but even so I could feel my body wanting more. He laughed.

"That's right. Get it down. Mind you were trying something, wanting to keep up with him."

I slumped back against the rock. I stared at the sea. He went and left me, I thought. The sod just left me. The man kept turning to the water, but he didn't move away.

"Inside job?" he said, and when I didn't understand, "You work inside."

"Aye. Yes."

"Not today, though, eh? You couldn't stand it, not when it's like this. You skived off, eh?"

I didn't know whether he was accusing me, or simply passing the time. I tried to laugh and make a joke of it. Sod you, I thought, when he started his yelling again.

"Little buggers. They just please themselves. I don't blame you, kid. Done it meself in me own day. What'd you say you do?"

"We're making a museum."

"Oh aye?"

"Aye." I remembered what Norman had said and how he had impressed me so much. "It'll show our heritage. It'll show what's been done here. It'll have fragments of everything we've achieved."

He smiled as his little girl tugged at his legs. She kept telling him to come on, come on home.

"Yes, my pet. Everything that's dead, you mean."

He stared, waiting for me to argue, and when I was silent he looked back to his other children, two boys and a another girl, who were trailing slowly across the sand towards us.

"I know," he said. "Old pictures. Proggy mats and pitmen's lamps. Bits of ship. The old days. The bloody old days."

He knelt beside his children when they came. He dried them with a massive towel and rubbed cream into their cheeks and shoulders. He cursed them as he did it, but his hands were so careful with them, so gentle.

"Poor sods," he said, kissing them each in turn. "Even the digging won't be left to do. Go on then, up you go."

He watched them climbing the first flight, then turned his back to them. I couldn't tell whether he was going to attack me or to cry.

"Look, son," he said, "I made things. I made things that sailed right out past here. Ships and rigs, setting out. And there'd be hundreds up on that hill there, watching, cheering fit to bust. My work. Cheering my work. Watching it go out. Understand? Aye? You? You're making nothing. A museum? They've got you digging graves. You're chucking it into a hole and wanting to jump in after it yourself." He crouched and gripped my collar. "Can you not see it, son? They've even got you talking dead man's talk. Heritage, achievements, what's been done. Well?" He peered into my eyes. "Well?" I stared back. I could smell the stale home brew on his breath. Sod off, I thought. Get back to bloody mothering your kids. He sighed and let me go, tucked his carrier under his arm. "Skiving's right, son. Keep out of it." He started to grin again before he went away. "And take those off, eh? Your mate's got the right idea. Strip off, swim out, sod it all."

Hating him, I watched him going up. What did he know? He was past it all, getting old. Redundant. Like my dad had said, the word meant useless. Things were changing, and he was bitter because they'd left him behind. What use was stripping off and swimming out if you wanted to keep up? I watched all the men leaving the beach. They were worn out by the sun and their children. Their bodies were brown but their eyes were red with disappointment and too much beer. They were half-asleep, half-dead. What could I learn from them when it was them with one foot in the grave?

I bought more lemonade from the cafe and lay outside waiting. I watched the tide slowly coming up, the shadow slowly going down. The breeze had turned and I felt colder and colder. I pulled Mickey's overalls on top of mine. The men with loudhailers had long ago come down from their chairs and they sat inside, talking in loud southern voices. Students,

I thought in cushy summer jobs. I'd give them something to do. I went to the door and said,

"I think I know somebody that's drowned."

They looked at me as if I was some kind of freak.

"Two of them," I said. "They went out hours ago."

"I mean it," I said.

I picked up one of the loudhailers and we went outside, down to the water's edge. They just stared out stupidly. I could see they thought I was messing them about. I lifted the loudhailer to my mouth and said,

"Mickey. Mickey."

The noise echoed round the cliffs and brought people running to stand beside us and ask, What's wrong, What's wrong?

"I mean it," I said. "They were on the rocks when the tide was out. Now there's nowhere for them, and they haven't come back. So what are you going to do?"

One of them shrugged and pulled off his t shirt. He waded into the water and began to swim quickly towards the headland. While he was out an old woman with a pink rubber hat stretched over her head put her arm on my shoulder. It'd be okay, she told me. The rescue services were wonderful now. When he disappeared I could feel her trembling as she whispered, "Don't worry, son. It'll all be fine." As he came back, everyone splashed out to meet him. He came out with his hands held up at the stupidity of it all.

"No problem," he told me, with a big grin on his face. "All they said was, Come on out as well."

He took the loudhailer and went back to the cafe with his friend. I could hear them beginning to roar with laughter. "You see?" the woman said. "You see?" Others came to congratulate me, then the crowd dispersed. I cursed them all. I cursed Mickey and I cursed his girl. What do they know? I thought. All this is nothing to do with them. He's from Bangla Desh or somewhere, like his snakes and tigers straight out of the bloody jungle. She'll flaunt herself to some rich git and get him to see to her. They think they're out of it. They think it's all just crap, but what they got that's better? Bloody big tattoos and suntans and gold bikinis. What good's that going to bring them, eh? They know nothing. Nowt. Sod them. Sod them all.

I thought of leaving, but I went on waiting. Miles out, a massive ship steamed south. The tide was bringing in plastic bottles, sandwich wrappings, dead weed. I heard the shutters on the cafe slammed down. I thought of home, my parents expecting me, the trouble there'd be if they found out. I should have gone in, I thought. I might have wasted it all. And what do you do if you waste your chances? What do you leave yourself?

"Mickey," I whispered, wanting to scream at him, "Mickey."

I took off the overalls and threw them up onto the beach. The water was icy. It took me minutes to get in and once I got started it was like I'd already been swimming for days. I was clumsy and sore and I could see hardly anything for all the splashing I made. I kept thinking I was going under, that I'd have to yell for help. But slowly I rounded the corner to where their beach had been.

The beach was gone. They were higher up now, sitting on a ledge with their arms around each other. I half-swam, half-scrambled from the sea. I tried to shout to them but all I could do was gasp and cough out water. I was climbing towards them when Mickey leaned over, grinned down at me.

"Daft sod," he said. "Here, get my hand."

He hauled me up and they shuffled aside, letting me in, making no move to cover themselves.

"He said you'd come," she told me. "I'm glad you did."

She was smiling at me, and was even lovelier than I remembered. I tried to answer her, but I was useless, embarrassed by her nakedness. I hunched awkwardly at a distance from them, and didn't know where to turn my eyes.

"Fancy sending out the guard," he said. I could hear the amusement in his voice.

"I waited ages. I thought you'd drowned."

He laughed. I kept my head turned away from him. I stared at the green moss that covered the ledge, at the rock face that was filled with scratched-in names and dates. I told myself, Get out of this.

"You think too much," he said. "Relax. Take your things off."

"I just came to see you were okay."

"We're fine. Come on. Nobody can see."

"No."

I felt his hand on my arm.

"Come on, Rob."

I think I'd have left then, just let myself tumble down into the dark water, but the girl suddenly said, "Leave him, eh?"

She pulled him back towards her. She pushed him until he was lying face down on the moss, and he laughed, letting her. With my face burning I watched as she began to trace with her fingers the long curved outlines of his tattoo. She winked at me.

"Ignore him, Rob. He's just a savage, not like us."

She started to talk about herself. Her name was Sharon, and she was our age. All the time she talked her fingers moved on him and he laughed softly, shifting from side to side.

"Schemes?" she said. "I started one as well. They put me in a hospital laundry. Sometimes you had to scrape the shit off the sheets before the machines would take them. Or the guts. I got to hate all those people upstairs, lying down and dying. I kept thinking about the kids back at school, lining up to take my place. We were checked in every morning and out every night. They made you put your hair in nets and your feet in rubber boots. Every Tuesday two jerks with degrees sat on a desk and wanted to know if we knew what johnnies were and which way we wiped our arses. One Friday I took my boots off and chucked them in the machine. They said they understood, they wouldn't get rid of me for that. It was my age, they said. I had to learn to fit in. Fit in a box, they meant. Sod that, I said. I'll have to get rid of myself, then. Bye bye. Sod you."

"It sounds terrible," I said, as she giggled at the memory. "We get nothing like that. Ours is okay."

Mickey's laughter spluttered at that. "Oh aye?" he yelled, but she cuffed him and told him to settle down.

"He told me you liked it," she said.

"It's better than nothing."

"Aye? But nothing's okay, Rob. Nothing's fine. Sign on, get the giro, go to the beach."

I shrugged, and looked down at the moss again. Beneath it the water was swelling, slapping the rocks. I was exhausted, and just wanted to leave. So drained, that even my embarrassment was gone, I could get no more pleasure from her beauty.

"Mickey," she whispered, "He thinks I'm a waster."

"No." I shook my head. "Sometimes I wish I had the guts to do the same."

Mickey twisted his head towards me.

"Like hell does he," he said. "He's a worker. He thinks it'll all be different for him. Don't you Rob?"

"I don't know. I don't know."

Sharon leaned across and put her hand on my shoulder.

"It's all right," she said. "He told me something else today. He told me how he wished sometimes he was more like you. He told me how he loved you."

"Watch," she said, when Mickey was face down again. "Watch how he shivers when I touch him here." She giggled as the muscles on his back rippled and the air burst from his mouth. "See? Go on, try it."

I hesitated, but she took my hand and put it on him. I let it rest there, then I let my fingers run freely over the brown scales and the coloured scales. I touched the tongue and the teeth and began to follow the coils towards the small of his back. I hesitated again.

"Mickey," I said, "What's it like getting this? How much does it hurt?"

"It's nothing. A bit of pain at first, then it's over. Go on. What you stopped for?"

I continued, until the ripples came again and his whole body stiffened.

"Ha!" he said. "Not bad, but not so good. What's wrong?"

I'd pulled my hand away. I sat shivering with my knees tight on my chest.

"I don't know. Nothing."

The sea was rocking, sending icy spray at us. The shade was like winter, the moss like frost.

"I shouldn't have come. I won't be able to get back."

They were both on their knees. I glared at them

"I won't," I said. "I won't."

I said, "You bastard, Mickey. You've ruined everything."

I tried to pull away, but she reached out again, put her hands flat against me.

"You're freezing," she said. "Sunstroke. You were out too long. Come here. Come on in."

She pulled me gently, and they shifted apart, letting me crawl between them.

"That's right," said Mickey. "That's better. You'll be fine now. Just relax."

They put their arms around me and come in close. When they felt how wet my trunks were, they helped me off with them. I felt their heat, their gentleness. I tried to tell Mickey how sorry I was, but he just said no, don't worry, it was nothing. We lay an age like that, watching the sea and sky change colour, sometimes whispering about the day it had been. Soon my body changed, stopped trembling. I found myself thinking of the overalls turning in the waves, my parent's rage, the lads gathering in the town, but all I could do was smile. Lying there under the priory with nothing on, being warmed by Mickey and his girl, I knew that I'd be able to get back, that everything would be fine, that till the sun went down there was nowhere else I'd rather be.

# After the Abandoned Wharves

After the abandoned wharves, the demolished warehouses, the streets of already-deserted homes, Michael skirted the high fences of the Marina, crossed the waste land, came to the entrance to Balmoral, where he shuddered, came to a halt, stood dead still in the silence, the early morning heat. Balmoral. This place. This hell. Why did they make him enter here, morning after morning..?

Deep cul-de-sacs, rings of pebbledash houses with desolate greens at their hearts. At the entrance, sprayed massively in red across the road: NO. BALMORAL SAYS NO. The worst streets, always the worst streets, for all the years he'd been coming here. Every other letter a final demand or a summons. Hardly a window left, plywood where the glass should be. Streetlights that had failed years back. Two year olds in nothing but scruffy vests running round in packs. The Armstrongs and the Askews and the Gladstones, screwing round at will, so the whole place had turned to one big crazy clan with the craziness getting worse at every breeding. Where for every kid hauled out and into care another two were born. Two more savages. Two more little beasts. Like their dogs, these people. Wild, and getting wilder. Dogs. The big brown get in 36, massive snout and a mane like a lion, that you never heard coming, knew nothing of till it was at your back with its gob snapping and snarling. The ones that waited behind the door till you were shoving the letters through, then went on like they were coming out the flap at you, tongues and teeth rammed up and howling at the opening. Alsatians raging at the windows as you entered the garden. Dobermanns that even the owners were terrified of, keeping them half-choked with steel chains and building cages - bloody cages - in the gardens for them. Ten stone Rotweillers that'd eat your own kids if you turned your back on them. They called them defenders. They said they needed them. They called them guardians, protectors, pets. He shuddered again. He'd heard the talk of worse, devil dogs or dragon dogs or something coming from the States. One of the guys had sworn he'd already seen one on his rounds. Teeth like blades, he'd said. Killer's eyes. Chained to a clothes post like a bloody bear. And when it saw you, and started thrashing and howling, like something straight out of a nightmare, heading straight from hell...

He stood there, staring in. How'd it come to this? How'd they let it come to this? He'd seen it way back, years back. There's trouble comin, he'd said. There's bother festerin in there. But they'd done nothing, gone on doing nothing, and the more they'd done nothing the more the whole place'd turned to jungle, crazy people and wild dogs all shacked up together, feeding off each other, whipping up each other... And now they'd tried to shift them and found it was too late, the wildness ran too deep. They wouldn't shift...

They'd been on TV, grunting about their rights and their intentions. They stood there in a semi-circle at the entrance and you could see the effort it took to civilise themselves. You could see the clenched fists, hear them gulping back the curses and the screams. What's this Marina to the likes of us? they asked. Why should we move for it? Where would we go? To hell, whispered Michael, squatting on the floor beside the screen, pointing to individual faces. That one, he said. And that one, look. They're the ones, love. Knife you quick as look at you. Animals, he said. You don't know the half of it, love.

Alison leaned over, touched him on the shoulder.

But look at the children, she whispered.

He looked. Unkempt things with mocking faces. Half-human things. He knew them, he'd seen them.

Angels, she whispered. Little innocents.

Michael laughed. Innocents!

Oh, love, she whispered, and she knelt by him.

We could take one, she said. Foster one. We could love one, Michael. Look at that one, Michael, that pretty one.

But look closely, love. There'll be paws where her hands an feet should be. There'll be hair runnin down the spine.

Oh, Michael.

It's true. Look at the fathers. Look at the eyes on them. Look at the sluts of mothers.

Oh, Michael...

We should brick them up. They'd soon be at each others' throats...

She pushed him away.

Just a matter then of sendin the bulldozers in, turnin them over into the rubble. Kids, dogs, whole soddin lot of them...

Stop it, she told him. Stop it..!

Nothing moved. Dust from the sites had settled on the roofs, in the gutters, in the uneven joints between the paving stones. It had settled on the house walls themselves, amongst the tiny pebbles, making them paler, bleaker things. The gardens were bleached and cracked by this summer's endless heat. Through the gaps between the houses he saw the river glistening, the cranes, the long-promised wonderful constructions: apartments and offices that would look down upon new plazas and new quays, upon bright sails dancing in the breeze. Everywhere the billboards showed how things would be, how this place would wake up soon into its brighter morning... The Marina. He grinned. Get it built. Get it over with. At least they won't bring devil dogs to the Marina. At least they won't end up screwing their own kids in the Marina...

A bony labrador moved out onto the road. It lay there sluggish, head resting on its paws, and even from this distance he saw the pink tongue hanging down, heard the panting. He shuddered again. He opened his sack, looked in. Bills, circulars, Readers' Digest nonsense, garish promises of excitement and wealth. He scanned the houses, saw no one but a little girl perched on a front step, and no one but she and the dog watched as he turned and walked away. So what? He'd known men take whole deliveries home, do their own personal sorting over a bacon sandwich and a cup of tea. Nobody had come to harm. Nobody had noticed anything had been missed. The man had a morning off, the good mail got delivered next morning sharp. Nobody but the postman had to bother with the junk... He'd tried it once, wandered in on her one dark February morning with his bag stuffed full and a grin on his face. Much good that had done him, the way she'd gone at him. Decency. Honesty. Caring for your fellow man. You know I'm right. Michael, you know I'm right. You don't know these people, he'd replied. You don't know what beasts they are. If you saw...

That had been an age before the Marina nonsense, an age before their own nonsense. These days when he walked away he ditched Balmoral's mail in skips and half-demolished buildings. He slung it out into the river in stone-weighted carrier bags. Then he'd wander through the sites, peer at the billboards, watch the future taking shape. Later, at home, he'd catch her staring.

Are you all right, Michael? she'd keep asking. Are you all right...?

His route led him to the waste land behind Balmoral, where the burned-out cars were, where the kids had dug deep trenches, covered them over with nicked corrugated steel so they could sniff and snort and screw in peace. He watched for dogs coming at him from the trenches or behind the cars. He picked up a snapped-off car aerial, ready to protect himself. But there were none nearby, only some mongrel a hundred yards away, engrossed in butting something dark and bloody in the earth, tearing at it with its teeth...

"Mister... mister!

The little girl, in long grass, the dog at her side. She stood with her arm around its neck, her face level with its jaws, and her eyes were filled with fright..

"Please, Mister!"

He didn't move. Little blonde thing, maybe six years old, her frock pink and filthy, her hair knotted and wild. He imagined Alison, how she would reach down to such a child, touch shoulders, cheeks, hair, murmuring of loveliness, how she'd come to him later, whispering that it wasn't over. They could adopt a child, foster a child. He clenched his fists. Bastards like these, breeding, breeding...

"Please, Mister! Please!"

"What?" he said, harshly, but restraining his urge to swear at her. "What?"

"Come an see, Mister." And when he still didn't move, "Please. Oh, please."

She led him through the grass. The ground sloped here, down towards a stream that trickled from a concrete pipe into a steep concrete-sided channel leading down towards the river. Above them, the back gardens of Balmoral, a bank strewn with rubbish, pocked with little excavated caves. Tangles of bedsteads and shopping trolleys. There'd be rats here, nest after nest of them. The air was loud with flies. She kept turning to him, beckoning him as they descended. The heat and stench intensified. What could she want him for?

They came to the final slope, six feet of concrete that dropped steeply to the stream. She stood at the brink, precarious, pointed down.

"There! Look, Mister. Down there!"

It was at the stream's edge, half in and half out of the water. A small sack tied with string. There was movement in it. Thin whining noises were coming from it.

He turned back to her, stared.

"Get them, Mister. Get them out."

The dog stood stupidly, tongue hanging slack, dripping.

She reached out, took his hand, tugged at him.

"Mister... Mister..."

He could hardly breathe down here. The heat, the awful air.

"You can do it, Mister." Encouraging him, persuading him. "It'll be all right, Mister."

"You bastards," he whispered. "Breeding, breeding..."

His head reeled. He recalled the consultant's office, how he had leaned down, pressed his eye to the microscope, stared down into the light... The sperms spun frantically, getting nowhere. They lay malformed, headless, tailless. They lay scattered, simply dead. He felt Alison's hand on his shoulder, heard her voice as she drew him back. Oh, love, she whispered. It'll be all right. There'll be something we can do. There must be something we can do...

"Please, Mister. Please!"

The consultant watched him. An infection, he said. An accident, maybe. At some time, something had gone wrong. Something that may have seemed trivial, hardly noticeable. Was there anything? Did he remember anything..?

"Mister!"

He raised his hands, a gesture of abandonment. He let the mail fall into the grass. He dropped to hands and knees at the edge, began slowly to swing himself over. As he let himself down, awkwardly braking his fall with feet, belly, knees, she urged him, soothed him.

"Go on," she told him, and he let himself fall, ended on all fours in the stream...

The water was icy cold and clear, sparkling as it trickled from the mouth of the pipe. All around the mouth were ferns and creeping plants, trails of star-shaped blooms. Bright mosses were rooted on the channel. A brilliantly-blue damsel fly hovered there, above the tiny waterfall. The air was cooler, reflections of water danced in the shade at the side of the channel, on his bare arms. He looked up, saw the dog's head and the girl's head, the fervent eyes poised over him.

He turned, reached out towards the sack, but hesitated. The whining in there, the movement. With fingertips he gripped the string that fastened the sack, quickly tugged it clear of the water, and he crouched, staring.

"Let them out," she told him. "Mister! Let them out."

He slid his hands under the sack and lifted it. He felt the weight of the animals inside. He felt their desperate limbs, frantic hearts. He felt tiny teeth and claws seeking an exit as he fumbled with the string, but he too was in a panic. He too was frantic, useless.

"Oh, Mister! Oh, Mister!"

He lifted the sack higher, held it up in both hands towards the girl and she reached out to take it from him, lifted the sack over the edge, turned from him...

He crouched again in the stream. He cupped his hands, lifted water to his head and face. He saw the damsel fly, still hovering. Beyond it, beyond the ferns and mosses at the mouth, lay the blackness in the pipe beneath Balmoral. He trembled. He remembered nothing. He foresaw nothing. He imagined the world above him razed, bulldozed, bleached, the sun glaring on the last few mutants, the final twitches of life. He imagined heat, brightness, immobility, going on forever. The thought of such damage, the thought of such a hell inside himself...

"Oh, Mister! Mister! Mister!"

The voice was singing, echoing down into the channel.

"Come see, Mister!"

She was leaning down to him, offering her hand to him, and as he scrambled up the slope, shoved himself onto the grass, she tugged him, helping to drag him over.

The sack was open. The puppies were tiny, beige, almost yellow in the sunlight. They sprawled exhausted in the grass. The dog stood over them, nudging them, licking them. Michael knelt speechless, found himself wondering at the beauty of the pups, the ugliness of the dog, found himself gazing into the girl's face, seeing it so transfigured by delight.

"Aren't they so pretty?" she said. "Aren't they so lovely?"

She took his hand, rested it on each of the puppies in turn.

"We saved them," she said. "Didn't we, Mister? Didn't we? You an me an Sabre! We saved them."

"Yes," he said. "We saved them."

He watched her with them, saw how delicate she was with them. He reached out to her, touched her shoulders, cheeks, hair.

"Yes," he whispered. "You an me an Sabre. We saved them."

She began lifting the puppies, trying to lay them in the crook of her arm, but she was too small, there wasn't room for them.

He slung the mail across his back, crooked his own arm, lay the puppies down on it, hushed them, soothed them.

"What will you do with them?" he asked.

"Just take them home. Look after them..."

She led the way, retracing the narrow path they'd worn through the long grass, and she kept turning to him, smiling. The dog followed, close behind. They heard the noise of children and their dogs coming from the gardens, the far-off noises of the sites. Above the river the cranes had begun to move across the sky.

They came back to the trenches and the cars, and as they approached the entrance he found the girl at his side, with her hand resting in his.

She led him in, and as they walked over the red writing he saw faces at the windows, watching. Children paused in the middle of their games. The dogs were out, roaming from garden to garden.

Somewhere a man was calling.

"Anna!" he called. "Anna! Anna! Anna!" The voice echoed through the cul-de-sacs, across the greens, over the roofs.

The girl laughed.

"That's me," she said.

"That's Dad," she said.

He thought of the mail. He should deliver it now that he'd returned, but her hand, tugging him forward, was insistent.

"It's just down here," she said. "Just through here, Mister."

One of the fully-boarded places. On every board the red word NO. Still the man was calling, but from another house, another street. "Anna! Anna! Anna!" She led him to the back of the house. The garden there looked out across bare flattened earth towards the wharves. The fence was reinforced with thick stakes hammered down into the grass. Tangles of barbed wire were nailed there. Rows of vegetables were growing, fruit bushes with tiny berries becoming visible amongst the green.

"Anna! Anna! Anna!"

The voice was troubled now.

"They think I'm gone," she said.

"I'm here!" she yelled. "Here I am!"

The back door was ajar. Michael laid the puppies in the grass, pushed the door further open. Breakfast things on a plastic table, the dog's bowl beneath. Behind the boards the windows were unbroken. He went in, shoved open another door, let light into the pitch-black living room. A few chairs arranged in a ring, at the centre a handful of eviction notices. Pasted on the window, newspaper reports of Balmoral's fight. On a sofa: a hatchet, a screwdriver, some carving knives.

Again she was calling.

"I'm here! Here I am!"

Her father's voice was closer.

He pulled the door shut, turned towards the garden. Sabre was in the doorway, teeth bared, growling.

"Sabre!" he said. "Let me out, Sabre!"

"Anna!" he said.

There were footsteps at the side of the house. The dog became excited, began barking, howling, began coming in.

"Anna!" he said. "Anna!"

He saw the man arrive outside. He saw him lean down and lift Anna into his arms.

"Anna!" he said. "Anna, Anna! Where've you been, my love?"

She started giggling, dancing in his arms.

"For the puppies," she said. "Me an the postman an the dog!"

And she pointed in.

"Look! Look who I've brought home!"

And as he turned, Michael looked out in wonder from the darkness into the father's joyful eyes, while Anna just laughed and laughed, saying,

"Sabre! Stop it, you silly dog..."

# Where Your Wings Were

For a long time after Helen died, mother used to pull my shoulders forward, kiss me, and slip her fingers beneath my shoulderblades. "You as well," she'd whisper. "Just like Helen, you as well. This is where your wings were. You left them behind when you came here. But be good, and you'll have them back again, one day."

Helen was an angel. One of those that God takes early. She was too good to stay here long. She died in infancy, flew straight into God's arms.

At night I tried to imagine her there. I lay in my bed, closed my eyes, tried to dream of her. I told myself that if I did see her, then it wouldn't be dreaming. It would be real. I whispered her name: "Helen. Little sister, little angel. Let me see you again. " But it wasn't to be. With my eyes closed or with my eyes open, all I could see was the darkness spreading all around.

As I grew older, and could feel the goodness leaving me, I tried to pray to Helen, ask her to intercede on my behalf, but the words appeared to go nowhere, and they brought me no comfort. Often I fingered my own shoulder blades and tried to imagine my wings, tried to imagine the feathers, bones and muscles known only to angels. But my fingers encountered my skin, my flesh, my bone: a simple human shape, nothing more. I searched my memory, tried to remember being there myself, so that I might try harder to return. I retreated, went back and back, remembered further, further, tried to imagine being inside my mother, then the time that preceded being inside my mother. But I could go no further than when I was an infant of two, maybe three, certainly before Helen came. My first memory was nothing of note, just me sitting in a pushchair staring up at my walking mother, and my father at her side. I believe that we are in the garden, have just come through the gate. My parents are so tall, so dark, silhouetted against the blazing sun. I see my mother lean towards me, smiling. "Look at him," she says, and I hear their gentle laughter. "You all right, my little angel?" she asks. I feel her light touch on my cheek, hear the first words I remember, naming me as an angel.

Before that moment, it is as if there's nothing. I do not exist. Trying to go back only emphasises my going forward. I become older. And as a boy, as I grew older, I felt the goodness leaving me, felt myself heading further and further towards a terrible dark.

It was painful to lie there failing to imagine Helen, with my parents sleeping in the room next door, and to feel the time of dreams approaching. Dreams. There seemed to be nothing I could do about them. I didn't want these things, I didn't encourage them. I didn't even have to imagine them. They just came out of the night, out of my skull. They came at me, night after night after night.

I confessed these dreams. At church, I knelt in front of the screen and told Father O'Mahoney about them. He was an old man with a gentle Irish voice that never seemed to criticise anything. I knew he must have heard everything before, but I wanted him to get angry, to shout at me, to warn me of terrible punishments. But he just listened and whispered,

"Yes... Oh, dear now... Yes..."

And then he forgave me, told me to pray for purity, and gave me a penance of Our Fathers, Hail Marys, Glory Bes. It was too easy. Even as I said the penance, kneeling at the altar rail, I knew it would happen again, and I wanted to be punished for it properly, before it became worse.

The dreams of course were about women and girls, about any woman or any girl who had caught my eye during the day. Naked women filled my thoughts and dreams. Naked women whispering and giggling. How was I able to imagine such nakedness? Probably I formed them from books of myths, geography books, engravings of ancient martyrs. I tried to avoid such sources of temptation, but as I quickly turned the pages or ducked my head away, I was aware that in my mind they moved with an intensity denied them on the page, that at night I alternately recoiled from them and welcomed them, and knew that whatever my daytime intentions were, each night I became more lost, more entangled in temptation.

In the effort to displace these dreams, and to supplement the inadequate penances of Father O'Mahoney, I spent many of these nights bringing to mind the awful day of Helen's death. Midsummer, an unblemished morning, sun streaming in at my window, a chorus of songbirds, silence in the house. Still early, 6 a.m. The thrill of holidays, the day before me stretching endless and unused and filled with hope. And then movement, my mother rising, her awful, awful cry. My poorly sister wouldn't wake, couldn't wake, was already gone to God. My mother pursued her, called after her, begged her, gripped my sister in her arms and refused to relinquish her. A whole morning of prayer and protest and lamentation, till such silence, and despite the sunlight such darkness, fell again. The doctor was allowed to confirm my sister's death, Father O'Mahoney to pray over her. I stumbled from the corner, mother let me and my father enter alongside my cold and long-gone sister the protection of her arms.

The dreams changed. One night my head was filled with a kind of fluttering. I turned towards it and saw an angel landing in my dark. She came towards me, floating rather than walking. She was clothed only in white fire, and her wings stood high behind her, covered in pure white feathers, like those of doves. Through the fire I could see her body, shaped like any woman's, but more beautiful than any woman's. Without speaking, she came to lie on me and I felt her fire all over and inside me. I lay stunned, watching her wings beating gently above us, pure white against the dark.

I told Father O'Mahoney. He listened in silence. Then there was concern in his voice.

"The tricks of the devil," he said. "They will adopt the most exquisite of shapes. Resist them all. Be firm."

I said my penances. But I was far gone. I knew that my angel would come again, that again she would be wonderful, the most wonderful thing I'd known. Night after night she came to wrap me in her fire, and I welcomed her, embraced her, though I knew she was leading me to hell.

One night, after she'd been lying on me for hours, her wings began to beat more quickly and I felt myself being raised. I held on tight, gazed into her perfect face as we began to fly through the gentle winds of the dark. She kept looking down at me, smiling to reassure me. We travelled for an age, until the dark began to change and we entered a pink dawn that slowly changed to white until the light itself was her fire, and she was so absorbed by it that I could no longer see her. I knew she was there only by feeling her tight in my arms, and by the continued rhythmic beating of her wings. I looked from side to side, wanting to see where we were, but there was only the fire on all sides, going on for ever.

I woke in my crumpled bed. There was frost on the window, snow outside. I closed my eyes tight, wanting the angel again, but I was awake, it was ordinary daylight, and she was gone.

I didn't confess it. I told myself it was just a dream, nothing to do with becoming bad. I just told the old dreams, the old women and girls. Father O'Mahoney said,

"Remember that the body is God's temple, and each of us is forever in God's thoughts. Keep yourself intact."

The next time, it started like snow falling, a thousand flakes falling from the darkness, each flake a glowing white flame. Then I saw the wings, and beneath the wings the bodies, each one a woman's, but more beautiful than any woman's. A whole flight of angels landed in my dark.

The angel I knew came to me first. Then the others one by one came to join her, until there were a thousand angels on me, and wherever I turned was filled with their white fire, their tender faces, their brilliant bodies, their beating wings.

We went together, all of us, through the winds of the dark, a fiery swarm with me at the centre, until we entered the pink again and then the white. They peeled away from me there, leaving me the one blemish in all that white. I threw my arms out frantically, striking wings and faces and breasts and hair, until my hand was taken and the angel drew me towards her and laid her arm across my shoulder.

"Don't worry," she whispered, and I could tell by the way she spoke that she was smiling. "There's someone to see you."

She took my hands and stretched them out into the brightness. My fingertips encountered skin, hair, eyes, a tender cheek. I felt the lips part, felt breath breaking into laughter.

"Helen," I gasped. "Helen."

I reached down, I lifted her, and at her back I felt the quick fluttering of her own small wings. She put her arms around my neck and kissed me and spoke my name.

"Oh, Helen," I gasped.

So much more I wanted to say. So much more I wanted to cry out. But I became speechless. I could only hold her, feel her as happy any tiny as she always was, feel the life continuing to burn and sparkle in her.

"You see?" she said, and her voice was filled with delight. "You see? I'm all right. Everything's all right."

Then she was gone, suddenly, flying out into the light and I knew there was no way to follow her.

"You see?" the angel whispered. "You see?"

"But how..?" I said. "How?"

She pressed a finger to my lips.

"Come with me," she said. "But never say a word."

We moved forward, and the white fire burned even more brightly, so brightly that I had to close my eyes against it. When we stopped, she whispered,

"Listen."

I could hear nothing, only my own breathing and the beating of my heart.

"Listen."

I started to ask what I should listen for, but then I heard it. Further into the fire, someone else was breathing. Long breaths in and long breaths out, filled with low groans, soft rattling and whistling sounds.

"Hear it?"

"Yes."

She turned me away, and we went back, to where I could open my eyes again.

"What was it?" I asked.

"That was God, fast asleep. He'll wake up soon. Hold on tight."

Back we came through the pink and the black, and into my room's darkness where we came to rest. She giggled like Helen had, and held me at arms' length, preparing to leave

"Don't go," I said.

"Everyone will wake up soon," she said.

"When can I come back again?" I asked.

She touched my cheek and smiled and shook her head.

"One day," she said. "When you have your wings again."

And then for the last time she lay on me, and the white fire that did not burn spread far into me, making me understand how it feels to be angelic. Then she was gone, diminishing to a snowflake, disappearing into the dark...

That day mother did again what she so often did. She pulled my shoulders forward and kissed me.

"You're the bright one this morning," she said.

I laughed. I let her slip her fingers beneath my shoulderblades.

"Where my wings were," I said. "Where they'll be again."

She held me close.

"It's true," she said. "Even though you're growing up so fast you have to keep on knowing that it's true."

I reached up and for the first time slipped my fingers beneath her own shoulderblades.

"You as well," I told her.

"Yes, me as well. All of us. Helen, you, me, all of us. Everybody."

And then we were silent, and we felt for a moment the fire within us burning, until father came, and we giggled, imagining together the white feathers rising from his hairy back and beyond his balding head.

It was the first time I had asked Father O'Mahoney anything, and it was the first time he became angry.

"If we're like this when we're in God's thoughts," I said, "What are we like when we're in his dreams?"

His hand struck the thin screen between us. He shouted at my blasphemy and gave me five decades of the rosary to say. I didn't say them, though. I knew that God slept, that even angels weren't always good, that I'd have my wings back one day, and that dreams were only dreams.

# Dogs

"Let's kill a dog," says Paul.

"You wouldn't," says Lee.

No answer.

"You wouldn't."

Night has fallen. They're in the space behind the houses, sprawled in the dirt. They can't see each other, not properly. The traffic's a low distant hum, houselights are on, mothers are calling. Behind them is a flat field of waste, years of waste backfilling the quarry, tussocks of weeds beginning to grow there. It's spring, and there's nothing to go home for. They watch dogs prowling, and want something.

"That one, look. We could have had it."

"Ha."

"Strangled it. Easy."

Paul imagines dogs. He's seen them eating him, beginning at his throat. He wakes inside dogs, howling.

"Do you not think of it - when they go for you? The ways you could do it. Pulling their jaws apart, or strangling them. Or just using a rock to break their heads in."

"No."

"I do."

"Stupid."

Soon after it started, his father came in. "We've got a little woof woof," he said. "Come on, little woof woof. Time to get up." He held out his belt like a leash. He threw him scraps at the table. "Come on, little woof woof, sit up and beg." He sat up and begged - how long ago? He still sits up, begs. "It's only a joke," his mother says. "Only a joke. Come on, just for fun."

One got him once, right in his own garden, came over the wall straight at him and lay on him, its jaws open and slavering. Terrified, he lay there screaming. But now...

"Anyway, it's like my dad says. You should care for dumb animals."

"Ha."

Paul turns, sets off into the field. Lee follows him. Beyond the field there's nothing - the wooded hill, more fields, roads that turn back to the estate. Sometimes they throw stones at the rats out here, but that's nothing.

"Where you going?"

"They'll see us, won't they, if we stay here."

"I'll have to go back anyway."

"Go back then."

They crouch behind tall weeds, in a depression in the ground. Lee turns the rocks over, scratches in the earth. He collects things, cleans them, displays them in his bedroom. Bottles and bottletops, bits of old china, curiously marked stones. He says the quarry's a goldmine - all kinds of precious things in it, if you knew what to look for. One day he found a whole skeleton, a mole or something, that had collapsed as he picked it up. But he took it anyway, and keeps it in a little heap in a saucer.

Stephen watches, can't see the point of it.

"Anyway," he says, "Who cares what anybody says."

Lee shrugs.

"What does it matter, once you're away from them? You've got to start doing what you want."

"Yeah."

"You're still just a kid, aren't you? Think you know everything, but you know nothing, do you?"

"Yeah."

"Some women like dogs."

"Women?"

"They like them. They shag with them."

"You're stupid you, if you believe that."

"You know nothing. They shag with them. They get babies with paws. They don't let on, but the babies are there, in hospitals."

"So how do you know, if they don't let on?"

"My dad said. He knows somebody that's seen ."

"Bet he didn't say shag."

"I knew what he meant. Shag. Shagging."

His mother had been there. She just laughed when she heard it. "Paul," she said. "You shouldn't say such things. You know what kids are." "Why not?" his father said. "It's true enough. Just getting him into the ways of the world. Aren't I, son?"

"I don't believe it," says Lee. "How could they? A dog wouldn't know what to do."

"Ha."

"It wouldn't, though. Think about it."

"You ever wanked a dog?"

"Wanked it?"

"There's no difference. They're like you and me, son."

Well, it wasn't him who had done it, but he had seen it. After a while they didn't even have to hold it down. It sat straight up with its tongue out and its head rolling, growling. It was smaller, that's all.

Lee's found something. He holds it up, wanting the light to catch it.

"What's that?" says Paul.

"I don't know. It feels like... I don't know. Can't see." He stands, puts it into his pocket. "I'm going home," he says. "Come on." Paul doesn't move. "My mam'll go mad."

"Mine won't."

Lee shrugs, and walks back towards the houses. Paul waits, then hurries to catch him. He grips his arm, makes him stop.

"We'd just have to pretend to be friendly," he says. "Get it to follow us into the fields. It would be easy. Nobody would see."

"Get lost."

"Who would know? We could get one of them that's always running about. One that was nobody's. And we could bury it."

Lee pulls away. At the edge of the estate, in the lane that leads between the back gardens into the street, he stops. He takes his find from his pocket, rubs it against his clothes, holds it to the light. He sees that it's nothing, flings it back into the field.

"You think you're special, don't you?" says Paul.

"Cos I won't kill a dog?"

Paul stares at him. It's not just that, but everything.

"Yeah," he says. "Cos you won't kill a dog."

"You do it then. Look, there's one. Go on strangle it, like you said. Go on."

Paul doesn't move. Lee walks to the end of the lane, turns towards home. Paul hears him, shouting back.

"You're stupid, you."

It's not only those that prowl. It's those that might be waiting, in the shadows of gateways and gardens, even with the streetlights on, and with men on the street, and their laughter. With his friend gone, Paul imagines their low scuffling movements, keeps in the light, crosses from pavement to pavement, his eyes straining. He thinks of daytime, and of their carcasses, all of them, piled in the roadway, steaming.

At home, his father's sleeping. He's slewed on a sofa, his hands gripping his groin. His mother, in her nightclothes, says,

"Where've you been?"

"Just out."

"Out?"

"With Lee."

That makes things right, he knows.

"It's been dark for ages."

"Yeah."

His father comes out from it.

"Leave the lad," he says, and grabs the boy, begins wrestling with him. He pulls his head close to his lips, to the heat of his breath.

"Been out in the dark, eh?" he says, threatening. But he laughs, releases him. Paul stands, rearranging his clothes, ready to leave them.

"He's no pup now, you know," his father says. "Look at him. He's got the scent in him, haven't you, lad?"

"Paul," says his mother - reproachful, but grinning.

He goes out, closes the door on them.

In his bed he lies hours, trying to imagine how he might do it, how he might strangle one, or use a stone from the field to crush one. But he can't see it. After a time, from the room next door, he hears his father's growls. He closes his eyes tight, blocks his ears, wants daytime. Soon he sleeps, enters his dog. He'll wake howling.

# Beacon Hill

I saw love for the first time on Beacon Hill,and my father called me forward, saying,

"What you gawping at, Petey? Hurry up."

I couldn't tear my eyes away. I saw the girl's knees above the bracken, the boy's buttocks in between, his purple-shirted back, his head bent ferociously to hers.

"Peter! Come on!"

He saw, or was determined to see, nothing. He walked on with his left hand held out behind him, reaching for me.

"Petey!"

And it was only when the boy had heard, and had turned his familiar face towards me, that I ran forward and let myself be hauled forward to my father's side.

Each Sunday that summer we walked from the village to the hill's crest. The lanes led us to turf and then to the concrete surface of the gunsite, to waist-high bracken and fern. The air was filled with the ringing of bells and the call of larks. All the way the wind rattled in stems and leaves, and all the way my father implored me to,

"Imagine it, Peter. Just imagine it - Beacon Hill, a town ablaze with light."

It was a small thing to imagine. Everyone had seen how things would be, scaled down to fit the newsagent's window: in the centre the village as it was, but with its roofs mended, its walls scrubbed clean, its gardens neatly fenced; all around it the new places, clusters of houses arranged in rings, squat blocks of flats facing playgrounds, shopping places behind long glassy walls, new schools placed onto acres of perfect green. Curving through it all were the new red roads that carried shining cars, that were edged with trees and mothers pushing prams, and that all made junctions with the dead straight gash of black descending from the crest.

I'd stood at the window with him for the first time months ago. He crouched close, his nose against the glass, his head level with mine. It stunned him into minutes of silence, until he gasped,

"Imagine it, Peter! Just imagine it!"

We walked on. He kept my hand contained in his. At the top we didn't turn as usual to see how much during the last week things had changed, to see the multiplying foundation trenches, the sites like little fenced-off craters spreading through the fields. He drew me forward across patches of heather and scattered rocks towards a horizon filled with roofs and spires and stacks, to where the ground dropped again and, "Look!" he cried. "They're even working today. Just look at it come."

Far below us was the new road trailing out from the city. Its route was ripped through cornfields and hedges. Closest to us were the bulldozers resting in their trenches of bared earth. Behind them was the long strip of yellow underfill, supporting steamrollers and dumper trucks. Further away, the yellow gave way to black. That was where they worked today. Dark and scurrying, bearing shovels, the men leaned into the smoke of their machine, tending the fire between its wheels while it inched forward, big as a house, pulling them closer, leaving the steaming black behind.

"Let's go down," he said. "Let's watch them."

I hesitated.

"Come on."

He led me down by a hawthorn hedge whose berries already were shining from dead bloom, in which twists of silver paper still marked where that spring's nests had been. He walked carelessly, letting cowparsley and rosebay spring back to cover my clothes with petals and seed, until a field of high barley separated us from the men. We peered through the hedges, he exclaiming at the power of it all, and when I complained of being able to see nothing, he swung me up onto his shoulders. I parted the tips of the trees, saw smoke, men hurrying across the flames, caught curses and laughter, the stench of burning tar; and when one of the men saw me, stretching to full height and swinging his shovel in recognition, I smiled shyly back, and waved, and asked to be let down.

"Navvies," he told me as we reascended. "Navvies, Peter. It's those lads that built us and made us strong. He showed me the fingers of his two hands knitted into a double fist. "Everything joined, you see, linked together. Canals first, then the railways, now roads. Everything joined so that it couldn't break, so nothing could make it break. And it's starting again, all that joining, despite everything they tried to do to us, despite everything they threw at us."

By the time we reached the crest again, he had talked himself into his familiar tales of war, of Beacon Hill blacked out, mother dead still and praying as the bombers droned in from the sea. He held me tight again, let his free hand sweep generously out towards the landscape. It was all here, he told me, all here: the persistence of the village, its new noise and future light, weeds growing where the guns had been, the sea's calmed horizon.

"Take it in, Peter. Make sure you take it all in. Watch it grow with you." And then he laughed, and leaned down to embrace me. "It's envy, son, that's all. If only you knew what a time you'll have."

And we went down again, and I was free to scan the bracken. It was becoming brown, it rattled in the wind, and it was empty.

"Keep still, lad. Won't you keep still?"

That evening my mother knelt by my side. She spoke through the pins gripped in her teeth. She snapped down my sleeves, turned up the cuffs to the level of my wrists.

"And keep straight," she said. "You'll get out no quicker by jiggling about."

"Anybody'd think you'd be proud," she said.

I sighed, watched the window, let her have her way. Half past eight and it was almost dusk. Behind me a fire burned, its heat painful against my bare legs.

"There. Now let me look at you."

She pushed me away and crouched on her haunches.

"Fasten it up properly, then. That's right." And she smiled, the noise of laughter caught in her throat. "Oh, Peter, put it all on. Go on, it won't take long."

I stood there.

"Go on."

In my room I stripped off my shorts and pullover and put on everything: the socks and flannel shorts, the pale shirt, dark tie. I tied on the heavy shoes. And I replaced the blazer, the too-long, too-wide covering of black with golden battlements shining from its pocket.

"Oh, Peter," she exclaimed when I returned. "Oh, Peter. What a man."

I ran out afterwards, released. The air was dead still. Smoke hung in the village, a hedge-high mist had risen on the hill. Lights were being turned on, and above the black crest, the sky was bronzed by the city. I hurried through the narrow streets, hesitating only at The Fleece, where I stared through the window into its single crowded room, saw my father in a corner raising his hands in argument with his friends. A hidden piano was being played, a coarse voice singing a sweet song followed me as I moved away. I went out of the village into the darkness of a cinder path at the allotments' edge, where the hawthorn crammed closer and the fences were high. That's where Jacker jumped out at me with his hissed,

"What's lads up to out here on a Sunday night?"

I threw him back. He let me pin him down, lean right down until my face was touching his.

"And what were lads up to our here on a Sunday afternoon," I replied.

Giggling, we rolled apart and hurried to where the cinder gave way to the hard cracked surface of the gunsite. Almost lost in the mist, we crept to our hide, the gunners' shelter, entered by steps down into the concrete, by a collapsed steel door. Inside we lit candles, hunched on brick benches. The mist had streamed in after us, and it fell through the light to the floor. I took out the cigarettes stolen from my father's pack and we smoked. Jacker put his hand to his groin, and rubbed. He said,

"Ooh, she said. Ooh."

"Bloody hell, Jacker."

"She said, Jacker do you think we should. She was dying for it. I said, Come on, eh? You like me, don't you. Come on."

"Shite."

"Ha, I brought her here and she said, Ooh I can smell something, so I took her outside and when we got started I kept saying, It's all right, you like me, don't you, nobody can see. And I got her all worked up so she was dying for it and she kept going, Ooh, ooh."

He watched me. I shook my head, muttered curses.

"But you bugger," he said, "I thought you'd spoiled it. Who is it, who is it? she said. Keep down, I said, I know him, it's all right, he hasn't seen. And you went over the top and I said, It's okay, he's gone. I was sure she'd want to stop, but she let me get on with it. We finished it fast, I sent her home and I came in here. Just as well she didn't look and see him with you, though. Ha, and you holding his bloody hand."

"Ha, he wouldn't let me go."

He laughed and sprawled back on his bench.

"See?" he said. "I told you. Didn't I say she would? Didn't I say she's just like the rest of them? She was dying for it, Pete. Dying. And she was lovely, Pete. Lovely."

"You see?" he said.

"Yeah." I nodded. "Yeah."

"Ha, he's my mate, I told her. And I told her about you and she said, Ooh. I could fix it, Pete, if you like. Get her up here for you. She'd come, Pete. Eh?"

I said nothing.

"Just think, eh? Getting it at your age. Hell, younger even that I was. Eh?"

He came closer, and began fiddling at my pullover. He threaded a brass paper fastener into it, a love button, held in the material by its two legs flattened out behind. He took my hand in his and rolled it into a fist, then pushed his index finger deep into my closed palm.

"Come on, Pete, eh? Just think, eh? Imagine it."

"I'd to get through the dark somehow if I was to get to her. Wi' not a torch to help, you know. Not even a match allowed. Isn't that right, love?"

My mother nodded and smiled, indulging his tipsy reminiscences.

"Ha, we'd get round Burma easier than I got round here. Took half the night to get over that hill. Always late, every time. An' the state I'd be in! Remember? Shoes soppin wet, jacket ripped half off me back by the damned hedges. Eh? Still," he said, leaning closer to me with a conspiratorial whisper, "Shows she must've been worth comin for, eh?"

I nodded.

"Love," he whispered. "That's what it's called. Love."

I sat wedged between them on the sofa. With their arms linked behind my head, we had spent many nights like this these past weeks.

Indulged with late suppers, I was the focus of their recollecting and foretelling, their stories of a love that had preceded me and that would continue after I'd left. My leaving: like war, love and light, it was an endless theme.

"What's this thing here?" he asked, suddenly raising his voice as he parted my hair with his fingertips. "What is this strange thing here? Brainbox, that's what, box stuffed with brains. Listen: I'm sittin in the pub tonight. I'm sittin there with farmers and navvies, and I'm talkin and I'm sayin, Listen, the world's changin, it's not the same world any more, we're livin in the past out here. I'm sayin the world's the place for brains now, and they're hummin and hawin and sayin, Aye mebbe you're right, and they bloody know I'm right. And all the time I'm thinkin, My son. My son, the one with brains. And I'm thinkin, No. You won't see him in wi'the navvies. You won't see him for dust once his time's come. No, he'll be out there in the world. And a bloody good job too's what I'm thinkin. Am I not right, love?"

"You're right."

"Course I am. Look at it. Bloody stuffed wi' brains."

She laughed, and I felt her fingers scrabbling with his in my hair.

"But what about the outside?" she asked. "Look at that for a state. There'll be no bed till that's been scrubbed tonight. What you been up to out there, lad?"

In the kitchen she filled a bath for me. She stood in front of me fingering the love button.

"What's this?" she asked.

"Just something I found."

"Oh," she said. "Who were you with tonight? Jacker?"

"Just Jacker, yes."

She clicked her tongue, but smiled when she saw that I was waiting for her to leave. From the doorway she said,

"We'll have to stop these nights, you know. There's just a week to go."

I lay in the water and looked at myself. I tried to imagine myself in Jacker's place, lying on top of the girl in the bracken, but Jacker stayed in his place, I in mine, holding my father's hand and walking to the crest. "She'll cross the button for you," Jacker had said. I looked at it, fastened to the wool by two legs that lay flat, away from each other, and I tried to imagine the act that would make them cross.

"Those brains can do anything," my father would say.

They couldn't do this.

He wore tight jeans and long pointed boots. His black sideburns were razed off at the jaw. He rested back on his elbows and stared towards the sea.

"Anyway," he said, "You won't even want to know me then."

I lay close beside him, absent-mindedly measuring myself against him. Though my head was level with his, my feet came only to his knees. I sighed. He had said all this before, ever since the results had come through, and I was bored with it.

"Tell me about the girl," I said, grinning, trying to change him.

"They never do, buggers at that school. Talk like teachers and dress like bloody priests."

I snorted phlegm into my mouth, spat it out in a long arc to my left.

"Not me, Jacker. You know that."

"Who knows?"

"I know."

"Yeah."

"What difference'll it make? There'll be nights, same as now. Who else is worth bothering about round here?"

"There'll be lots. Fancy buggers doing their homework then going out to sniff the flowers. You'll find them."

"Fuck off, Jacker."

He turned and stared at me.

"Don't tell me to fuck off, Pete," he said.

"Never," he said.

I lowered my eyes and rolled away from him. I stared down, into the turf. For minutes we lay like that, and the hill seemed filled with noise: the roar of heavy machines, rattling of drills, ringing of handtools. Somewhere a jammed gearbox screeched and wrenched.

"You're stupid, man," I said. "Stupid."

He came at me then. Half astride me he pressed my face into the grass. He pushed until it seemed my nose would break. Then he was away. I watched him going down, kicking the undergrowth. I touched my face, tasted the blood running into my mouth.

"Fuck off," I yelled, looking at nothing. "Fuck off."

"That's right. You tell him, lad."

It came from behind me. I turned to see an engineer twenty yards away, aiming his theodolite across the concrete. Behind him they were laying posts in straight line from the crest. He came towards me asking if I'd been hurt. I shook my head and hurried back down.

Mother was in the garden with a neighbour. They sat on chairs with enormous enamel bowls in their laps, shelling peas.

"We're not ready for it," she was saying. "Not us that were born here and stayed here."

"I know," said her friend, turning to include me in her audience as I slipped in through the back gate. "It's doing it all at once that gets me, making it all so new so fast. Just look at this one."

Mother laughed.

"The states that lad comes home in. But he'll be the fine one next week, just you wait."

"Indeed he will."

"Go on show us, Petey, eh? Go on, put it on."

"Leave the lad. You can see he's shy of it."

"He's all right. Go on, Petey, eh?"

I fixed a smile on my face, walked straight past them, through the house and into the street. It was lunchtime, silent. I moved through the centre. Outside The Fleece navvies sprawled on the grass. I was stiff and angular as I passed by with my eyes fixed on the horizon. A couple of them barked at me in play. Another called,

"Now couldn't I put a sweet one like that on my shovel to fry."

I saw nothing of Jacker that week. I stayed close to the house and the garden. I was sitting on the back step trying to draw the hill when I saw the bulldozer come over the crest. By the next afternoon it was at the gunsite, and it rested there while men with pneumatic drills broke through the concrete.

My mother kept asking,

"Are you all right, son?"

She kept saying,

"It'll be all right, you know. It'll be fine. You're going to love it."

One of those days my father came in from work, saying,

"I saw your Jacker out in town today. Not seeing him now?"

I shook my head.

"Aye? But that'll be the way of it now, I suppose. What a size he's getting, eh?"

"Yeah."

"Wouldn't like to cross him in a dark alley in a few years time."

"He wouldn't touch you."

"Aye, I know. I know the lads like him. It was them that got us through. He'll be grand, now there's work for them."

Evenings we sat together with the radio on, and they joined in with its songs, laughed at its jokes. It kept telling us of a cold war, making my father curse.

"Mebbe we should have gone on with it," he said. "Mebbe we should have ended it, properly. We might have known it'd be like this."

When he left for The Fleece we sat in silence, I with my pyjamas on. While she darned and sewed I pretended to read, and let the inadequately-formed image of Jacker's girl stir and confuse me. Each night I went to bed early, when the sky at my window was hardly black, wanting to dream her. Each night I told myself next day I'd go and look for her. Sunday came, and he took me onto the hill again. Outside the village there was only a hundred yards of turf before the trench began. We walked into it past the resting machine. On either side were heaped earth, concrete, ruined hawthorn, that damped the noises of churchbells, wind and larks, and the trench was so straight and so deep that I could only see out of it by turning back towards the village and the distant sea. We stumbled as we went up, our feet catching in rubble and the machine's tracks, and as always my father urged me on with his exclamations of astonishment.

"The speed of it all," he kept saying. "The bloody speed!"

At the crest we sidled past more machines onto the underfill. We looked over and saw that the black was halfway up the other side. Already one edge of it was beginning to be cleared and kerbed. The machine rumbled and flared, inching higher, and there was nothing left to stop us going down to it. We went to stand within yards of it. The air trembled, scorched our faces, was filled with stench and smoke. Its men were yelling curses and instructions to one another. They came closer, and we crouched, shielding our faces and holding our breath, but staring into the flames and the boiling surface of the new road.

"Hello, lads!" he shouted. "Grand job you're doing there!"

And they waved back with their shovels, grinning and contorted, their leather aprons, leather caps and florid skin spattered with black.

"Keep it coming, lads! Keep it up!"

I couldn't stand much more. I turned away, retching, and began to reascend. It was minutes before he followed me. He took my hand and I felt his skin burning. I saw the black spots on his trousers, the fire in his face.

We went back to the smell of roasting meat. Pans rattled on the stove. Mother was in the living room with the radio blaring, sending up steam as she thumped the iron across my uniform.

"It's bloody awe-inspiring out there," he told her. "Tell her what it's like, son. Bloody awe-inspiring, nothing less."

He stood in the back doorway, blushing. It was half-past eight.

"It's Jacker," she said, her lips tight and disapproving.

"It's too late," she said.

My father looked at me. I said nothing.

"I don't know," he said. "What do you think?"

I shrugged.

"I don't know."

I glanced towards the door. He beckoned me, a quick backward jerk of his head.

"Maybe half an hour, love. What do you think?"

She shook her head.

"Half an hour," he said to me. "No more, mind. Okay?"

I hesitated, watching her. She sighed.

"Go on, then," she said wearily, and when I didn't move, "Go on, get yourself away. But half an hour, you hear?"

My father's voice broke into a laugh.

"Go on, then. Anybody'd think you didn't want to go."

Outside, Jacker half-dragged me from the garden.

"Move," he said, and then he stopped and took me be the shoulders.

"She's coming," he said. "I got her to say she'd come."

The changed ground was difficult in the dark. We both fell headlong into the side of the trench, and we had to scramble on hands and knees until we reached the familiar bracken.

"That's better," he panted. "Clear ground. Come on. What's up with you? Move!"

We ran uphill, whipped by the undergrowth, to where the gunsite's edge had been. We stood there looking back to the village lights. He had a cigarette lighter. He flicked it on and off, on and off.

"I said I'd signal her. Watch for her, Pete, she said she'd have a torch."

We watched. More lights were switched on. None moved. The breeze was cold and filled with dew. I watched the disappearing stars, heard Jacker's breath begin to quicken again.

"Hope we haven't missed her, Petey," he said. "But no, too early for that. Watch for her, Petey, don't worry, she'll come."

He edged close to me and began to rub my shoulders. His hands felt huge, but awkward, timid.

"Cold? Aye, I know, but she'll warm you, Petey, I tell you she will."

He kept seeing what he thought was her, then seeing he was wrong.

"Shit," he said, when the drizzle came. "Won't come now."

His hands gripped me.

"Cow," he hissed. "All the same. Aren't they, Pete? Aren't they? Fancy buggers, aren't they? Go on, Petey, say something. Call her something. What you shaking for?"

I twisted free of him and set off running down again.

"Go on, then," he shouted after me. "Fuck off, then. You're all the bloody same."

I ran. I felt concrete and hawthorn cutting into me as I scrambled into the trench. I ran headlong into the machine. I crawled away from it half-stunned.

He caught up with me on the other side, and reached for me so clumsily that he spilled us both to the ground. He landed on top of me. I couldn't move, but had to just lie there with his arms around me restraining me, and with his face beside me flat against the turf. He was trembling.

"Jacker," I told him. "I've got to go."

He didn't move.

"Jacker."

I tried to slip my hand beneath his face, tried to lift it.

"She said she'd come," he said, the words deadened by the earth.

"It doesn't matter. It's nothing."

I twisted closer to him, laid my head on his.

"Jacker," I whispered. "Jacker."

"It was for you, Petey. Just for you."

I let him cry for a while. Soon I heard my mother calling me from the garden.

"I've got to go," I said.

We sat up together, and set off together towards the lights. Before we separated I put my arm around him, touched his face.

"Petey," he said. "What a state we must look."

It started us both laughing.

"Aye," I said. "But what does it matter, eh?"

I walked out that first morning wearing the brand new grey, white and black, with the gold battlements shining from my pocket, the leathery scent of the satchel following me; and with my mother watching, watching from the gate, waving furiously each time I turned to steal a glance. I walked through the centre past the newsagents and The Fleece, saw in each greeting from each familiar face an odd mixture of amusement and respect. The vans had begun to bring the navvies in, and as if I were a girl I became the object of their whistling and the noise of their horns.

I waited at the shelter, the one child in the line of those who travelled to the city for work. Between the houses and the building sites I saw the red roof of the bus as it made its slow way through the lanes towards us. It had arrived and we had begun to file aboard, when suddenly I heard him.

"Ooh, is that our Peter? Ooh, our Peter!"

He stood on the far side of the street in his tight jeans and long pointed boots, love buttons in intricate patterns on his purple shirt. He came across, grinning, hand on hip.

"Ooh, Peter, let me look at you."

Dead still, I let the others file past me. They sniggered, or told me to take no notice of the brute. I tried to smile as he came closer, but I couldn't hold it. I lowered my face, felt it burn.

"Daft sod," he said, and he took my hand, rolling it into his fist. "Just came to say good luck."

I looked up at him, and we grinned.

"Good luck, Pete."

Then he was away, running through the centre. I turned back to the bus, opening my hand to see the button he had left there, its legs crossed.

# Spotlight

It started as a game, in October, on the night the clocks went back. As usual, Anthony was playing on the green. As usual, I was watching from the window. There were simple games, ball games, skipping games. Girls were singing and chanting and their voices echoed from the houses all around. As it darkened, I watched them all huddle together, then I watched Anthony come back to the house. He wanted a torch, he said. It was for a new game. A game played in the dark.

"What game?" I whispered.

He sighed.

"Oh, mother." he said. "It's called Spotlight."

He stood there with his hand on his hip.

"Please," he said. "They're waiting for me, mother. Give me the torch and let me go."

I held my breath. I held his arm. I peered out into the dusk, saw the white expectant faces of his friends beyond the garden wall.

Stay inside, I wanted to say, but I couldn't speak. I saw Robert watching me, assessing me.

"Please," said Anthony. "You're hurting me."

It was Robert who found the torch, Robert who released Anthony,

Robert who sent him out and then turned to me, sighing, and held me tight.

"You have to stop clinging to him," he told me. "You have to stop scaring him."

"I know. But I didn't stop him, did I?" I pointed to the children heading out into the dark. "Look, I let him go."

Spotlight. It became the only game for night. Each dusk that autumn the children gathered at the centre of the green, around the monument that was their bay. They stood impatient, glancing up towards the sky, the multiplying stars. In someone's hand the torch flashed on and off, on and off. Each night they began early, when the day's light hadn't entirely left the sky, and rushed out towards the alleyways, garden walls and hedges at the limits of the green. Once they had settled and the squealing of the youngest ones had stopped, the only sound came from the one child left at the centre, who bent low with his head held in his hands, filling the air with the loud drone of his counting: "One... two... three... four..." Until at last with a cry of "Coming out!" he switched on the torch, left the centre, began a long search punctuated by wild screams of discovery, sudden struggles, frantic races to the bay.

Each night I watched from the window. I saw the white plumes of their breath, heard the high-pitched excited voices, the fearful laughter. I saw how the game dispersed and grew, and I knew how Anthony deceived me. Despite our agreement that the game should never go beyond the hedgerow at the limits of the green, that quickly became too tame for all of them. Each night I saw the torchbeam flashing further into the wilderness outside. And in the daytime, when we walked out there, where all the ancient pits and shafts had been, we saw how the ground was becoming riddled with hiding places, how the turf could be lifted in blanket-sized sections to expose the ancient ash and the impressions of children's bodies beneath.

Robert told me, "It's helping him to settle here. And you have to allow him secrecy. It's part of growing. He's fine. Everything's fine."

I told myself that he was right. It was just a game. There was nothing to fear. But when with the other parents I began to shout my child's name time after time into the dark, I never truly expected him to come back. But come he did, an age after I'd begun, with his clothes filthy, his hands and face scraped by twigs and thorns and grit, and with his eyes abstracted and wide, as if I'd called him back from an adventure, or from some astounding dream...

My own dream, of coming here, had formed a year back, when we lived in the city, that nightmare place. Garish noise and light by day, perilous dark at night. All around us were ruined streets. I saw needles and glue tubes, drained cans of lighter fluid scattered in gardens and gutters. In the shadows I saw beasts of men with bottles in their fists and slurred curses on their tongues. Damaged children huddled in doorways, slept in half-demolished houses. We lived behind locked doors, shuttered windows. We defended ourselves with fences and alarms and lights. I kept Anthony inside. I never let him go out alone into the dark. Robert told me I was stifling the boy. I must begin to let him go. I pointed from the window. Can you not see them waiting for him? I demanded. There, look. There and there and there. Constantly, Robert tried to soothe me. It was not so bad as I imagined, he told me: I saw only the dark things, only the bad. He persuaded me to see doctors who fed me tablets, recommended yoga classes, relaxation classes. They talked of an imbalance in my nature, that caused me to see my surroundings as vindictive. They suggested that perhaps another child... Another child? They saw nothing. How could we bring up another child there?

I saw further than all of them. I saw all the dangers. I saw into the city's dreadful heart, and then one sunlit afternoon, when I raised my eyes, I saw the gentle surroundings that might give us an escape. Beyond and above the city were the moors rising to the sky. So green, so calm, surrounded by such gentle light. That's where we should go, I said to Robert. To that green and peaceful place. We can raise our child there. We can give him his freedom there.

He held me tight.

Will it be better there? he asked.

Yes. Oh, yes.

We got out. We sold the house and came up into this lovely place. Here were small villages nestling on hillsides, green paddocks and hawthorn hedges, clean air and space and light. A revitalised place. A place that had been scarred for centuries was becoming pastoral again. We had more than half a year of contentment here: the spring given to restoring our new home, then the long summer of our own renewal, each day seeming further to disentangle us from the city and our past. Anthony threw off his memories and plunged into the freedom offered by this place, by all his new friends. I felt my own nightmares dispersing slowly, I felt something like joy entering my heart.

"It's healed us all," Robert would say, as we watched from our window the children playing in the sun. "We should have left years ago..."

We prepared early for winter, hoarding food and fuel. During our walks, we'd glance up towards the high Pennine horizon, anticipating storms. But late autumn, the first weeks of winter, seemed paradoxically to pass by in intensifying light: icy days without a breath of wind, the sun blazing low over the horizon, the dawns mauve, the twilights amber, burning into nights that sparkled with frost and stars. We lit our Christmas lights and for the first time understood that this festival truly was the celebration of life's flame burning in the dark.

I watched the colours dance across Anthony's eyes, and I told him, "You'll be so happy here. You couldn't have a better place to grow..."

On Midwinter's eve we gathered bright holly from the hedges. Walking back, we stopped at the centre of the green, Robert took Anthony's hand and pressed it to the monument's cold stone. He traced the date of the pit disaster, the column of names worn smooth by a century and a half of northern weather.

"Just think," he said. "Children on all fours in the dark. Crawling, never seeing daylight. If we'd lived then..."

I pulled their hands away.

"All that's over now. This place is peaceful countryside again. There's no more going down into the dark..."

But he continued, told us how they'd landscaped the pitheaps, blocked up the shafts. He said there were workings down there cut off since the disaster. He shrugged off my restraining hand. He smiled, so comforting.

"He has to learn these things," he said. "These things have to be remembered."

"You're frightening him," I said, but trembling out there on the ancient turf, I knew it was I who was scared, who gripped Anthony's hand tight until he told me,

"You're hurting, mother. Let me go."

That night I was woken by his screams. I went to his bed and his eyes were wild in the light from the bedside lamp.

"They're digging further down," he gasped.

He gripped me harder than he ever had.

"They're getting down to where the bones are!"

It took an age, but I thought I'd calmed him. I thought he was sleeping, and I was leaving him.

"Who's that in the light?" he yelled.

Next day, Midwinter's Day, at dusk, I held him back as he prepared to go out to the green.

"Anthony," I whispered. "Not tonight."

"Oh, mother!" he said, and I heard in his voice how tedious I could be to him.

He stepped out with the torch in his hand.

"It was only a dream," he muttered. "It's just a game..."

I watched through the window. I peered out through the tunnel of my hands. I saw the familiar gathering and dispersal, watched the lone crouched figure at the monument, and this time it was Anthony, his voice counting. He counted backwards, down to one and "Coming out!" He stood erect, and switched on the torch, which suddenly deepened the darkness all around. Then he headed out towards the waste. For minutes there was only the beam lifting and falling through the tangled hedge and someone out there screaming.

Robert called me from the fireside: "What you doing? Come and drink something. Come and sit with me. Leave the boy alone."

The torchlight moved further out, was a thin beam moving vertically across the earth.

"Anthony," I whispered. "Come back in."

I went out through the back door, began to move across the green. Once more, someone was screaming. I heard Anthony coming back, heard him ripping the hedge in his need to break through. Then he ran with the light dancing furiously in his fist and a shadowed figure running at his heels. He was first to bay, and he retched, gasped, gathered his breath to go out again.

I stifled my cry, but the beam swung to me and caught me.

"Who's that?" he said: a deep whisper, menacing, amused. Then came his bitter, "What you doing out?"

"Where's the one who chased you?" I asked him. I ran, grabbed the torch, swung it in a circle around us: no one at the monument, no one on the green. "Where is he? Where?" I put my arm around him, tried to hold him. "What did you find out there?"

He shoved me off. In the glare of the torchlight I saw the rage he felt for me.

"What did you find out there? What was chasing you?"

"Oh, mother," he said, and then he left, cursing me, racing back into the night.

I stared back at the houses, their windows filled with hundreds of tiny lights. I cried, leaning on the ice-cold stone, and I switched the torch off and on, off and on. The wide circle around the monument remained deserted. Then I followed him. I crossed the green, crawled on all fours through the tangles of the hedge. Outside, in deeper darkness and on broken ground, I walked awkwardly, clumsily. All around me were shifting shadows, children sniggering. I crouched, shone my torch into the hollows, found nothing. I lifted the blankets of turf, and beneath them, in the light, caught nothing. I moved further out, and all the time I whispered, "Anthony! Anthony!" There were more hedges to push through, more pits to trip me. Soon the sniggering and the shifting stopped. The earth became more meagre. I felt the loose ash beneath my feet, tussocks of turf that had never taken. The village was tiny, a cluster of stars against the black. I'd come too far. "Anthony," I whispered. "Oh, Anthony." And at last, from miles away, from right back where I'd started, came his own cry: "Mother! Mother!" I turned quickly, tripped, fell flat against the earth. My palms were scored by the grit, I tasted blood on my lips. I cursed myself, reached out for the torch, and all around me the earth began to open, and they began to come out from their hollows and hiding places. Children, dozens of them, half-naked, pushing away the turf and grit with skinny hands, then coming at me with their scent of firedamp and death and their whispering, "Who's this? Who's this? Who's this?"

# Nesting

For years he'd pestered her: Tell me what it was like when I was in you. Tell me what it was like before I was here.

For years she'd told him. But as he grew older, he began never to ask. And she began only on bright mornings ever to tell.

It was spring. The streetlights were on. Blackbirds had stopped singing in the hedges.

"Stay inside," she said. "Just one night."

He perched on the edge of his chair, with his jacket on his knee.

"Stephen!"

It was her pleading voice, the one he hated.

"Just goin f'ra while," he muttered. "Not long."

"You'd protect me, Stephen. Soon as he went you said you would. Now I'll be the man, you said. The man."

"An' I will. Tellin y'I will."

"Tellin's nothin. Stay inside."

He crouched and fiddled with his shoelaces, fastening them viciously tight.

"They come through the windows, Stephen, even when you're in. Doesn't matter if you're in. They wait in the gardens for the men to leave. They come in quiet wi'their knives and snooker cues, wi'stockins on their faces. Woman keep still, they tell you. Not a move or you'll get what's comin. Where is it? they ask. Stephen, what'll I tell them when there's nowt?"

"So what's to come for if there's nowt?"

"That's it. What they left with? Me. Nowt but me. Stephen, stay inside."

"There's nobody, woman. Who'd wait to get in here?"

He followed the street's long curve, turned into the narrow alley that led him out through the fringes onto the waste. Out there the ground dropped, a sudden quickening of the miles-long slope towards the sea. Once there'd been a few streets here, almost a village. There were a few stone remnants blanketed by bramble and ivy, thin strips of garden still marked by rampant hedges. Spreading out from it was a circle of paltry spoil-heaps, and deep gashes in the earth that had become the estate's dumps. Years ago, with the other kids, he'd spend whole days roaming the hillside, searching the hedges for nests. The ruined streets had been their ghost town, where they'd play until the long scary shadows came and sent them running, filled with laughter and fright, back towards the brand new houses.

Now the other kids went other ways. They took buses into the city that was already burning the sky beyond the crest. They gathered in the estate's community centres and clubs. And, it was true, there were those who did prowl the curving streets, poised to take their chances.

He shuddered and went down, taking a narrow cindered track, ancient waggonway edged with its dense hawthorn hedges. He knew it all, even in the dark. After a quarter mile or so, he turned right, ducking through towards a cottage less dilapidated than most. It smelt of shit in there, and massive thistles grew out through the floor. But there were walls almost as tall as he was, with strips of bleached paper still attached behind the creepers. A single window frame remained, a square filled with the slope, the silhouettes of factories at the top, the burning sky. He lowered himself onto the collection of cushions and rags he'd months ago dragged from the dumps. He emptied his pockets: an aerosol, a plastic bag. He sprayed the aerosol until there was a pool in the corner of the bag. He wrapped the bag around his face and breathed deeply. He went on breathing, tightening the bag's opening against his cheeks, pushing his lips closer and closer, waiting for the darkness to deepen, for the thundering of blood to begin.

The day he left, she had Stephen singing. They sat together on the sofa, looking out into the street. Her voice started it:

"Clap hands for Daddy coming
Down the waggonway
His pockets full of money
And his hands all clay..."

She kept leaving him, scanning from the window, returning to him. She smiled. "Come on, Stephen. What's wrong? Too big to sing now?" She took his hands, clapped them between her own.

"Clap hands for Daddy coming
Down the waggonway..."

They went on waiting as far as dusk and beyond. He lay against her breast and felt her trembling. "Sing," she whispered. "Sing."

He sang. He was twelve years old then. He'd been born here, when the estate was a riddle of foundation trenches, half-made roads, half-formed walls. His infancy had been accompanied by the clink of trowels, the suck and smack of piledrivers, the bulleting of pneumatic drills. On expeditions out, strapped into the Silver Cross that lurched on rubble and underfill, he stared out from beneath the dark hood to watch his mother cursing, grinning through her sweat, singing at him, calling to the foremen, "Will it ever all be done?" She taught him the ring of streets, the alleyways out onto the slope, the wilderness outside, the distant sea. She showed him the factories being massively assembled around the crest. "That's where Daddy'll go," she told him. "When it's all done, he'll be in there, workin the machines." As he grew older, between the men going up in the morning and their coming back at night, he learned the dusty silence of the streets, the afternoons disturbed only by children playing, mothers calling, the endless droning from the crest. "And's how it ought to be," his father would say. "Whole places made for them like us. Homes put here, work put here. So's it's all clean and new and settled f'ra change, and you feel you're worth somethin wi' a life worth lookin forward to. Right, lass? Bloody aye."

Sundays he'd take Stephen out, leaving the Silver Cross to gleam uselessly in the kitchen. "Mother's stuff," he'd say. "The lad's got legs. May's well learn from the start which way they'll be leadin him." So the boy was half-led, half-dragged, with his arm held vertical by the man's fist, towards the new workplaces that even on Sundays were filled with the subdued beating of engines. Out here his father cursed freely, inviting the boy into a man's fellowship of work and sweat. "Tired, kid? I bloody bet y'are. T's how it is. T's how it's always been for them like us." He turned the boy's face towards each factory in turn. "But we're winnin, kid. We made our claim, an look!"

After the singing, long silence and the dark. Her body trembling, sudden outbursts of her breath. She clenched him tight, tighter, till he slithered from her grip with,

"Mam! I cannot breathe."

"Where's that man?" she whispered. "Stephen, go and look."

At the door he followed with his eyes the curve of streetlights, shadowed gardens, curtained panes.

She shouted at him, "Well? Well?" She came up behind him, shoved his arms into a coat.

"Thinks we're nothin. Thinks he can do it, like he said he would. Can't, can he? Can't get away with it. We'll find the bugger, Stephen, bloody right we will. Out you go. Come on, bloody out!"

Out through an alleyway onto the dead straight road leading to the crest, cutting across a waste of weedy underfill towards the darkened factories. Nothing but a thin whining from them now, padlocked gates, massive loading doors sealed shut. At his place, beneath its shattered neon name, the one light came from a shed at arm's length inside the fence. She shoved her arm through, hammered at it. From inside a man's voice yelled at her to clear off home. She went on hammering, until its tiny window was opened and he yelled,

"Is that still you soddin kids?"

"It's me," she told him. "Me. Look. Just me, an the lad here."

He angled his head through the open frame.

"What's wrong, woman? What you after?"

"Me man," she said. "I'm lookin for me man."

"Oh, aye?"

"I want to know who's workin," she said. "If he's workin."

"Workin? No bugger, only me. They finished ages past."

"But if there's another shift... If they needed one to get it done..."

"Look around, woman. Listen."

She pressed her face hard against the fence.

"Then where is he? Where's my man?"

The watchman stared at her. He sighed and spat.

"Go home, woman. There's more to worry him than bloody silly women an their kids."

The window slammed. They headed back to the estate. On the wasteland in between she picked up half-bricks, stones, and flung them out into the dark. Afterwards, they searched the pubs, didn't find him there.

Feathers and cotton clung to his skin. He drew his knees to his chest, squirmed into the rags. He was so cold. He would have to move.

He'd dreamed of going home one night to find her dying, the house ransacked, the bloodied snooker cue beside her head. But tonight was like most nights: opening the door to a room filled with the fierce heat of a gas fire, to her drunken sleep; leaving her there, going to stare from his window at the ring of lights surrounded by the dark; slipping towards unconsciousness again, towards the memory of his father, the last night he'd come in...

"Stevie! Stevie!" An urgent whisper, the man leaning over him, the door open to the landing's glare.

"Stevie! What's the matter wi'ye?"

Blinking, heart thundering, gasping for air.

"Stevie! It's me, lad. What's up wi'ye?"

"Nothin." A garbled cry.

"So what ye laughin for?"

"Laughin? Dream, dad... Must've been a dream."

"Bugger dreams, lad. Sleep, lad. Eh?"

"Yes, dad."

"No dreams now, eh?"

"No, Dad..."

The man turning to leave, but hesitating, pushing the door to, returning through the darkness to the bed. Crouching low, his lips hard by the boy's ear, his whisper cracking with its angry edge,

"This is how they get you, this is how they lie to you. Look at this, they tell you. Isn't it grand, isn't it what you've always wanted? Get you when you're daft, half-asleep, when they tell you, Good lad, always knew you were a good'n. Gan on, they say, Smile. Look what we've got you. Gan on, lad, take it... Bastards! Get you when you're dreamin, son, get you when you're soft. And not long till they've got what they wanted and they're telling you, No! Leave off! Get back to where you were! Back in your box, bird brain. Yours? Wors. Wors all the time. Not for the like o'you. Piss off back to sleep. Leave it!... You know what I'm sayin, son?"

Stephen lay as if he couldn't move, breathing low, his heart racing.

"Get out, Stevie. That's me meanin. That's the thing to do. Get out quick's you can. Soon as there's a space, start runnin. They'll try to stop you. Nice lad, they'll say. Always been a good'n. Come here, look at this, they'll say. Don't believe them, Stevie. Tell them, Stevie: Piss off wi'your lies! Aye? Stevie!"

Huge hands gripped Stephen's head, twisted it towards the dark face.

"Stevie! Tell me aye. Bloody aye!"

"Yes... yes... aye...," the words coming suddenly, on each panted breath.

"Good lad, Stevie. That's the way. When they come to you, just tell them no."

The hands relaxed. The face dipped towards him, kissed him.

"Good lad. You'll be all right. Just gan to sleep. That's right, son. That's right... love."

Nothing more, except, as the man moved towards the door, the final words, "An don't marry. Don't fall for that lot, either," and later, the ferocious voices of both of them, man and woman, stretching deep into the night.

"... an he'd lean over, from where you're sittin now, an he'd lay his whole hand flat across me belly - like this, look. Just to feel you. Just to feel the kickin of you. An he'd swear - you know, the way he did. Bugger, he'd say. Feel it growin, gettin strong. He'd keep on askin, How big's it, how big's it now? An when he'd had a drink he'd come an lay his head on me and he'd whisper at you and whistle for you. He'd be that daft - like a kid that cannot wait. Howay, little'n, he'd say. Howay out an play wi'us. You never knew him, Stephen - not when he was young and full of everythin. I've got it all, he used to say, an, Me an you, love, we've got it all..."

Mornings were calm, comparatively lucid. When the sun shone and the blackbirds sang, she'd lift a table into the small back garden and they'd breakfast there, facing each other, their knees almost touching. Her words each time searched the same themes: the past, his father, the building of the estate and the factories. But her stories had never become tedious to him. Though he never met her eyes, and hardly spoke except to mutter yes or no when asked if he, too, remembered, he was alert to every word, bringing as it did some answer to his prompting of years ago: Tell me what it was like ...

"...it was spring when you were growin fastest. Felt some days like you were takin all the strength from me, an all I could do was lie an let him fuss round me. Days when I was stronger he'd take me out onto the waggonways an we'd walk an walk, right down past the tips an dumps.

What a change there'd be down there, where you could lose yourself in the lanes an hedges. It was the silence of it all, when up here there was all day long the trucks an drills an engines. An wi'the plans they had, seemed like it would go on always, like there'd be no stop to it, like the estates would just keep spreadin and spreadin... But it weren't to be... Comin back, I'd have to hold him tight, let him take me weight. Take it easy, love, he'd say. An he'd let me stop an get me breath while he climbed right into the hedges lookin for nests an shouting back about the eggs an little'ns he'd found. An many's the time I came back here wi'a warm hedgesparrow's egg in me hand or a chaffinch's in me pocket..."

Her voice faded. Soon, he knew, it would deepen, she'd begin to search her other theme, of how it all went wrong. She held him as he tried to move away.

"We watched you growin straight an strong and he'd laugh an say, The jammy sod - born now, best of all times to be born..."

From inside, through the kitchen window, he watched her head fall forward. He shivered. She'd start on the bad times, the changes. "It broke his heart, Stevie. It changed him. It started him sayin we shouldn't've started any of it, we shouldn't've met, we shouldn't've come here. He started watchin you an sayin we shouldn't've had you, it might all have been easier if we hadn't've had you..."

"Stevie!" She had turned to him, and he saw that the morning's light hadn't entirely drained from her eyes. "An your eggs! You remember them? Boxes an boxes o'them underneath your bed. All that bright blue an the white an the dark patches. An how he loved you even then? How he'd sit wi'you an hold them wi'you and keep tellin you what this one was an this one was..."

"Aye," said Stephen, moving from the window, heading out. He did remember - the man's gentle touch as he fingered the hollow shells and the pinholes; how he turned his face from the boy as he muttered that this was maybe the best way,

"Spat out like so much snot - never to be born at all."

Some days he still went out like this, as if he were still dragged by his father's fist. He ascended the hill, passed the silent factories, squatted among the heather and rocks at the crest. He kept jamming a tin of lighter fluid to his nostril, squeezing. Icy-cold, breath-stopping, but with an almost immediate thrill that sent his mind reeling. The estate hunched in on itself behind back gardens and fences. The broken ground at its fringes contained trenches and heaps of underfill, remnants of long-abandoned building projects, weeds that each spring were higher and more dense. He saw his father's arms widening as he described what was to come, filling the space with houses and workplaces going on for ever. He saw his father in a rage, coming out from the factories, running to the crest, setting off on the miles-long ribbon of road towards the city, yelling, "No. Bloody no!" One day he'd follow him… Thin mucous was draining from him. He sniffed, spat. He'd said no, months ago. They'd come to him, wanting him for their schemes and projects, with, "He's a good lad, is Stephen. We'll train him. We'll give him what he needs." He watched them, silent. Lies, he thought. They were tender, telling him he'd change things for his mother and himself. She'd been with him, had turned to him, her eyes widening with anticipation. "No!" he'd yelled at her. "Bloody no!"... He spat again. He stood up, began his descent. All across the hillside the work of those who'd said yes was starting: neat signposts at the junctions of the waggonways, trimmed and newly-laid hedges, turfed spoil heaps. They'd get to his cottage, raze it. They'd clear the estate's fringes. There'd be playgrounds and picnic spots. On the crest there'd be parking places and benches. Children on tiptoe would peer through telescopes as far as the sea. You could be part of all this, they'd told him. You'll help the whole place to be re-born. People will want this place, will want to come. "Stephen," she'd whispered - her whining voice. "No!" he'd yelled. "Bloody no!"... He veered past the estate onto his familiar cindered track. He started when the hedge started. He ducked into the dark, climbed, balanced in the forks of the boughs, peered towards the tips, heard all around him the mothers, filled with fright, clattering towards the sky. Nests; so many of them, deep inside the foliage, held and protected by spreading twigs and branches. He stretched, reached up, dipped his fingers into the first: a blackbird's, with its smooth and cupped inside. Three eggs. He lifted them one by one, placed them gently into his free hand's open palm. For a moment he regarded them, their blueness, their dark speckles. For a moment he heard the familiar voice from below: In your mouth, lad. Rest it on your tongue where it's warm and safe. He closed his fist tight. He sniffed, wiped his hand on his clothes, began again. The nests he couldn't reach he brought down, kicking and wrenching the branches that supported them until they splintered and snapped. He moved slowly stepping from tree to tree, balancing, staring, reaching. All afternoon he worked. Occasionally he rested, squatting in a wide fork and holding the lighter fluid to his nose. Once, in a strong tree, he climbed so high that his head emerged from the foliage and he stared back, saw how short a space, compared with the miles of hedgerow that crossed the slope, he'd dealt with. But he didn't relent, went back into the dark, went back to leaving the ground and the branches scattered with smashed eggs, with young birds cheeping uselessly for their parents, went back to telling himself, "Better like this. Aye, better like this..."

At dusk, he dropped to the track. He marked the place with a pile of stones. He shuffled through to his cottage, curled up in there. His clothes were ripped, his skin torn. Tiny fragments of shell had attached themselves to every part of him. He took out the lighter fluid once more. Nothing left except a vapour. It brought no thrill. He didn't reel. But he slept, and entered a darkness deeper than any there'd ever been out here in the waste; darkness with the thudding of blood in it and with a voice from outside coming closer, asking, "How big's it? How big's it now?" and going on to call him, "Little'n! Little'n! Howay out an play wi'us..."

They hadn't come. There was no bloodied snooker cue. She was sleeping on the sofa, facing the gas fire. He stood staring, this boy coated with shell and feathers and with hollow eyes. He didn't want to leave, didn't want the whisper or the landing's glare. She didn't move. He turned off the light, turned off the fire, lay down with her. Without waking, she moved to accommodate him, allowed him to curl up close against her belly. They stayed all night. He kept waking. He kept promising her,

"I'll protect you, Mam. I'll stay inside..."

# 1962

These things happened so long ago. For anything at all to happen then, there needed to be the pretty ones, and there needed to be the beasts. There were Daniel and Askew, my friends; my mother, who was taken from us at the start; the tramp, who came soon afterwards to live in our dunes. And there was me, and there was my father, living somewhere in the spaces in between.

It started soon after she was taken. It was a Sunday. I was asleep, dreaming her, and my father's voice, from outside the house, woke me. I lay listening, trying to understand, trying to distinguish the other voice, the unfamiliar. By the time I was at the window, this other, with black greatcoat hanging leaden to his heels and the beret jammed to his skull, was leaving. He tucked a parcel into his khaki kitbag, stepped down onto the beach, didn't look back.

Downstairs, at the table, my father muttered at me, cursed me.

"Twice I called you. Twice you answered: I'm coming... Yes, I'm coming."

I remembered none of it. I poured honey from a spoon onto my bread, watched the trembling patterns it made beneath my dead still hand.

"Look at the time. You might as well have stayed up there. It's nothing to you, is it? Or if it is, then it's nothing but a dream."

I tried to turn away, tried to focus on the sea's horizon, but this was before he had learned that his terror could be silent, and he took my head in his hand, twisted me to him.

"Well?" he asked me. "Well?"

I said nothing, waiting for him to release me, and it was only when his hands fell to the table that I whispered, "Who was it, at the door this morning?" and he whispered in bitter reply, "Jesus Christ, Tom! Is that all you can come up with? Jesus bloody Christ!"

Before we left for the hospital, I slipped out to the gate. I crossed the track, stood above the beach, gazed north towards the lighthouse, south towards the docks. No one but the coal collectors and their ponies, the usual children digging in the sand, a dog, spurred on by its master, leaping at the waves.

On the bus, he sat with his arm round me. He smoked cigarette after cigarette and I felt his bursts of coughing, suddenly controlled. The bus was filled with a transistor's tinny noise, playing all the way to Newcastle, and each time The Beatles sang I felt the leaping of my heart, the desire to pull away from him, laughing. He was silent until we entered the city and he pointed down across the traffic. "Look," he said. "You remember that?"

"The Memorial," I said, and I blushed, recalling again the embarrassment he'd brought me the previous November, the way he'd stood stockstill through the praying and the hymns, the way his voice had rung out above all others into the surrounding silent streets. She'd been with us then, had stood behind me with her hands gentle on my shoulders and her singing calm and sweet. Afterwards, when he went to drink for an hour with his friends, she took me walking by the river. "Poor Tom," she said. "One day you'll understand. It was so awful, worse than anything there'll ever be again." And then she laughed, and kissed me, and said that we were free of all that, and on the bridges we loosened our coats, gripped our hats, raced each other, yelling, "Beat you to the other side!"

In the ward, we stood waiting for her to wake. He kept smoothing my hair with his licked palm. He whispered, "Don't let her see that we've been quarrelling so much." In the end, I leaned down to her, moved my fingers gently on her brow. "Oh, Tom!" she exclaimed, before her eyes were even open. "But look," she said. "You've grown so tall." She made me stand beyond the bed's foot while he held her forward. "Every time a little taller." And she smiled, a fading smile as he lowered her to the pillows again. "And look at me," she said. "Now I'm the little one. So tiny." I sat at her feet. She kept drifting to sleep, waking, scolding herself. "I can't seem to stay," she whispered, her voice now more breath than articulation. "What will become of me?" It was as if she was disappearing before our eyes. I wanted to reach beneath the covers, to touch her, to reassure myself that the ever-narrowing ridge beneath the covers was truly her. I'd already dreamed of finding nothing there, and I'd also dreamed of coming here at night, sitting on the starched sheets by her, telling her, "It's nothing. You're only becoming little again. You'll shrink to a baby's size and you'll start all over again. It's what happens these days. I'll take care of you." And I laughed and said, "Just look at the size of me!" It seemed so easy. Next time I dreamed she was a baby, lying asleep, her nightgown a vast christening robe arranged across the bed. I carried her away from the hospital and the city, brought her to our beach. I lowered her into the waves, shouted her baptism to the coal gatherers, and she came out wailing, filled with life.

As we were leaving, the Sister spoke to my father in her room. "The treatment," she whispered. "I know. It's almost another disease itself. But it's all we have to fight with." He stood with his head turned down, his fists loosely clenched at his sides. "Is there nothing we can do?" he asked her. "Is there nowhere else we can take her?"

She let her hand rest on his shoulder.

"You must let her see that you are calm."

"These'll be no good, you know," said Daniel, once Askew and I had finally wrestled each other breathlessly to the sand. We'd been racing, leaping the huge concrete cubes that lined the foreshore. "No bloody good at all," he said. The cubes lined this whole beach, lined all the beaches to the north. They were sinking, some of them were already half-buried in the sand. The only gap was at the centre of the bay, where the coal gatherers had dragged one of the cubes aside in order to make an entrance and exit for their ponies.

He stood with his hands in the pockets of his white shorts, his hooped jersey slopping down across his hips. He looked down at us. "There'll be no landing craft, no tanks. It'll be guided missiles next time. It'll just be an ordinary day - dead silent, and then..."

"Shut up, Daniel," said Askew, standing up, shaking the sand from his clothes. "You're talking shite. It'll not happen. Never."

Daniel just shrugged at that, said, "Ban the bomb, that's what I say.

And bloody quick, too."

Askew snorted, and led us off in the direction of the lighthouse. "Get rid of him," he muttered. "I don't know what you see in him." But I shook my head. "It's because he's new here. You'll get used to him."

It was mid-afternoon, high tide, and the beach was deserted. The water was hardly moving beneath a steel sky. We came to the little headland that marked the limit to our bay. Beyond it was the marsh and the little copse of pine trees, then the long stretch of higher, wilder dunes, where the pitmen's tiny, brightly-painted holiday huts nestled in the hollows. Behind it all, stretching back inland, were the villages and their dark spoil heaps, their pitheads black etchings in the afternoon's grey haze.

Daniel and I perched on the rocks beneath the lighthouse. Askew stood further out, grinning, thrusting his hips forward, pissing far out into the sea. Daniel inspected the surface of the rocks. With his small fingers he traced the inscriptions carved into the dark stone. He murmured names and dates. They were all around us, the deep inscriptions of the dead. "1902," he said. "1898. Tom - 1860! A hundred years, and still not washed away." I nodded, and showed him my namesake,Thomas 1882, Thomas 1905, the second written in a smaller, plainer script, and wondered again if the Thomases could be the same. Then Askew came, buttoning his fly, with his story of the stone beneath the water line, with a dozen Askews on it, going two centuries into the past.

"Two centuries," he said, and I saw the glare in his eye. "Two hundred years of being here."

Then he stopped, and stood staring back inland.

"Who's this bugger?" he whispered, and both Daniel and I stood to stare with him.

He was moving away from us, across the marsh. He was dressed as before - the greatcoat, the beret. The kit bag was lashed diagonally across his back. He moved awkwardly, attempting to keep clear of the more sodden places, but he kept sticking, and he had to keep pulling himself free.

"He came to our place, begging," I said.

We moved off the rocks, onto the turf that topped the headland. The man was clear of the marsh, had begun weaving his way through the pine trees. Soon he was into the dunes, and lost in them.

"He asked for work," said Daniel. "They let him help to dig the drains."

"Did they, by God?" whispered Askew, and again I saw the fire in his eyes, but Daniel continued,

"He was there all afternoon, breaking through to the old ones. Then they fed him, and sent him off with some bread and some cold tea. He stank of seaweed. They said he was half-crazy." He turned to me. "He was harmless, though wasn't he, Tom?"

I caught my breath.

"I hardly saw him. My dad gave him something, I think. Not much." I watched Askew. "What do you think?" I asked him.

He didn't answer, but just stared at me, then said suddenly,

"OK. Let's move."

We left Daniel behind. He wouldn't come. Askew cursed him as we splashed through the marsh. "You want to be careful, you know," he told me. "Swine like him'll change you." In among the pines I realised how the light was fading, how late it was becoming. "I'll have to be back before long," I told him. On the dunes the sand kept collapsing beneath our feet, and in places we had to climb on all fours, grip the sharp-edged marram grass, and when we rested I saw that my hands were crisscrossed by long thin lacerations, lines of tiny bulbs of blood. There was no sign of the man's footprints in the sand. "He could have gone anywhere," I said, looking past the huts towards the north, to where the landscape and the beaches became ever more barren, ever more wild. "What time will it be?" I asked him. He led me on. Each time we came upon a hut, he peered through its tiny windows, rattled its locks. "There's children come here in summertime," he said. "Don't want some old get like him lying in wait for them." But in the end he just stopped, and cursed, and stood on the highest of dunes with his hands on his hips, shouting, "Come on out, tramp! Filthy bastard, come on out!" I turned away from him and led the way back, tumbling down onto the shore, trailing towards the pines. All the way, Askew was cursing, saying, "We'll get the bastard. We'll drive him out." The tide was ebbing, the wet beach shone brilliantly beneath black clouds that streamed in from the horizon. As we approached the pines we saw Daniel, the white bloom of his shirt upon the rocks. Askew held me back, pointed to him. "Look at it," he whispered. "Little nancy boy, still waiting. Little girly, sitting on the rocks." I ignored him, moved in silence through the marsh. On the other side, he grabbed me, and his voice was thrilled, trembling. "Now," he whispered. "Let's get him now." But I pulled free, and soaked to the knees and with my heart thundering, I started running. Behind me in the dusk I heard Askew growling, Daniel's yelps of pain. But it was so late. Already the house was locked and empty. I followed the lane towards the village. At the centre, the small square of shops arranged around the fountain, I began to weep. The bus was leaving, was already heading out through the narrow streets on the other side. From the brilliantly-lit upstairs deck, a face I knew must be that of my father was peering back at me through tunnelled hands.

We were on the beach together, my mother and I, when first it showed itself. An icy February day with the whole sea churning. She kept pulling me to her, wrapping me round with the huge sleeves of her woollen coat, laughing at the absurdity of living in such a place. "He said we'd go everywhere!" she shouted, raising her voice against the din of waves and wind. She ran to the water's edge, tiptoed rapidly backwards when the water rushed towards her feet. She raged at the sea's coldness, its blackness, but her face, as she flung handfuls of sodden sand and coal into the waves, was filled with delight. "That man of ours!" she yelled. "What a fraud! It was to be Canada this, Australia that! Oh, yes, that was the style! A whole world waiting! Free as birds! We'll sharp be out of this hole, eh?" And she took my hand and danced me back and forth along the shore with, "Come on, Tom, my lovely Tom. Dance yourself away with me." She rushed me to the shelter of the cubes, and, "Look," she whispered, taking from her purse a tiny square photograph of herself, holding it cupped in her palms.The print had lost all whiteness, but she smiled out, beautiful, from beneath the darkening of all the years between. In it she was sixteen, and beneath the curls her face appeared an image of my own, as if she were some unknown sister, or some alternative version of myself. "This is the only me that's been, or's going anywhere," she laughed. "Silly man. He took it out with him to Egypt, carried it all the way back. Said he'd have done without tin hat or rifle before doing without that. Angel, he called me when he'd made it back. Guardian angel. And then he gave it back to me to keep it safe." I reached into her hands to lift it, but the wind rushed in between us, caught the photograph, sent it spinning out onto the open beach, and, "Oh, Tom!" she yelled, as I sprinted after it, "Oh catch it, Tom!" I caught it a hundred yards away at the water's edge. It was face down, clinging to the wet sand, and when I lifted it, already the dampness had begun to seep in from its edges. She welcomed me back with applause and, "How quick you are, my Tom!" but when she slipped the picture back into her purse, I saw in her eyes how truly scared she'd been. "It's all right," I told her. "It'll dry. It'll be just like it was." I took her hand and we stepped up onto the rough ground above the beach. The wind was clattering last year's weeds, was whipping at her coat. She kept stumbling. "Damned weather," she muttered. "Damned place. Hold tight, Tom. Hold me tight."

That afternoon I ministered to her. I carried warm drinks and blankets to her, heaped coal onto the fire, but I couldn't seem to warm her until I knelt and held her feet, tucked them beneath my pullover. We smiled at that and when my father came in, she was asleep at last.

"We went on the beach," I told him. "It was icy cold."

"Aye," he said, and with the back of his fingers he touched her brow. "She's sickening for something."

We sat silent, at opposite sides of the fire. At six-o-clock he switched on the television with its sound low. There'd been nuclear tests in Russia. In America, Kennedy shuffled the papers on his lectern, whispered quickly to one of his generals, then spoke of his resolution, of our growing strength. There were no limits, he told us, to the steps we'd take.

The voices woke her, and she stared at the two of us, her eyes filled with surprise.

"Fancy!" she whispered. "After all that worrying, being scared of losing everything, to find myself with all of this. I think I'd like to go upstairs now, my loves."

He went to her, lifted her, and we all smiled at her familiar lightness, her smallness. As he carried her out, she grinned back at me over his shoulder. She winked at me. "Australia," she said, and she giggled at the word. "Australia!"

While they were gone, I retrieved the picture from her purse. A wide blister of damp had spread across her face. I laid it on the mantelpiece, stood staring at my own face in the mirror above, imagined curls falling to my shoulders, imagined brave and teasing eyes. Soon he came to my side.

"It's a chill," he told me. "Nothing more."

He lifted the photograph. With his index finger he smoothed seasalt and speckles of coaldust from its surface. He laughed. "She said you'd have swum to Germany to get it back. Look at her, son. She was really something, eh?"

Later that evening the wind fell. The sound of the sea was a regular slap and hiss of small waves. He went on watching TV. I told him that I'd go walking for a while and he nodded, asked if I didn't mind if he didn't come with me this time. Outside, a huge moon had lifted over the horizon. Far out, the tiny lights of trawlers headed north. I kept to the lane, walking towards the village. At its edge I turned inland, to Daniel's place where I climbed the garden wall and crouched in the shadows, staring in. They'd installed a window that fell almost to ground level. Inside, the walls had been stripped back to the bare stone. Furniture and wooden crates were stacked against the walls. Daniel was perched among these, reading a magazine. His parents lounged on the single sofa, laughing, feet stretched out towards the electric fire. There was music, the complicated, incomprehensible sounds of jazz, and I watched Daniel nodding his head to it, swaying his shoulders. When it ended, his father stood up. He was dressed in jeans, a huge green pullover that covered his hips. He leaned over the record player, holding his hair back with his hands, and positioned a stack of singles above the turntable. Now I knew the wailed introduction, the insistent voices:

If there's anything that you want,
If there's anything I can do...

Inside, Daniel was dancing. I got to my feet and climbed back into the lane. The moon was higher now, above the centre of the sea, filling the surface with its light. I began to run, over the rough ground, over the concrete defences, onto the sand. I pulled off my shoes and waded through the water and its ever-present bits of swirling black. I tugged at my hair, twisted it around my fingertips. "It'll be just like it was," I insisted. "It will be. Just like it was."

The man had been again. This time I'd seen him coming. I was at my window, watching for Askew. I scanned the beach and saw him at the rocks. He came slowly, toeing the weed and jetsam. Occasionally he stooped to the sand, inspected something, lifted it, until he turned away from the water and headed for us. I saw him for the first time plainly, saw the black eyes in the white exhausted face, the lips a bloody gash between white whiskers, the hair hanging wild below the tight beret. At the gate, he caught me staring, and he hesitated. I edged backwards into the room, seeing the sudden lifting of his chin, his nod, his acknowledgement. Dead still, I listened to the muffled negotiations from below, returned in the silence afterwards to the window. From the lane outside, while he stuffed his paper parcel into his coat, he looked again, gave his acknowledgement again. My father came to join me, put his hand on my shoulder and we watched him moving on.

"Poor soul," he said. "Gave all he had and look what he's been brought to." He held me tighter. "What's wrong?" he asked.

"Nothing. It's what he could get up to, though. What he could do. There's children..."

He was laughing, indulgent, tender.

"What he could do? He hardly knows his own name, never mind how to harm. He was in Singapore, Tom. Any harm was whipped out of him years ago."

He took me downstairs, where he had soup waiting.

"It's not the likes of him that's dangerous," he said. "It's the others, the ones that came through and that've still got it in them. The ones that's waiting for the chance to start it all again. You can hear them anywhere, any day. Listen."

And he switched on the news, and sure enough they started, the voices talking of war, threatening war.

"This isn't enough for them," he whispered. "This peace, this quiet. Listen to them - animals, howling for blood."

Afterwards, we swept and dusted the living room together. I polished the window, staring through, watching for Askew. The air was filled with shimmering pinpricks of dust.

"We'll keep it lovely for her!" he exclaimed. "I'll carry her in and she'll say, Oh, haven't you been so good!"

I saw Askew coming through the lane. He had a long stick, he kept beating the weeds, sending the seeds high around him.

"She will come?" I whispered.

"Oh aye, Tom. One way or another, they'll send her home." And he came and hugged me so tight I was almost in pain. "And isn't that a day to look forward to?"

Askew didn't even ask me. He just told me we were going back into the dunes.

"Christ!" he said, striding on the firm sand by the water, "Have you seen him, close to? Have you smelt him? I kept my distance, but he's a fucking nightmare, Tom. And the stink of him! Like something rotten. Like somebody already dead." And in the marsh he stopped, stared down at the saturated ground, cursed again. "And when he was past," he said, "When he was past I was shaking. Fucking shaking. Like this, look. Just like this."

On the dunes, I saw that he was burning with desire. With his face inflamed, and his feet thumping on the turf and sand, he moved so quickly I struggled in his wake. We went further this time, to where there were fewer pathways and fewer, meaner huts. "This is where he'll be," he told me. "Keep your eyes peeled, Tom. This is where he'll be." We moved slowly. We prowled. I was trembling. I kept looking back, in terror of finding him already with us. But it was I who found his place, on a steep, landward slope of the dunes. I saw the driftwood, stacked high beside a charred hole in the earth, then the hut, a clumsy arrangement of floorboards and railway sleepers half-buried in the sand. Askew embraced me. "You're bloody beautiful!" he said, and he pulled me, led me down. The windows were shuttered. Inside, in the building's single room, by the light of the open door, we saw blankets drawn neatly over a timber bed. A spindly table, bleached almost white, bore a few crusts, a tin mug with tea dregs in it. There was a chipped enamel bowl by the door, some tattered magazines. Nothing more. I stood in the doorway while Askew went to the bed, lifted its covers back. "Oh, Christ," he whispered. "The stench of it." I moved further into the dark, smelled nothing but seaweed and damp sand, a lingering scent of creosote. "What is it?" I asked. He flung the covers right back, making gagging noises in his throat. "Can you not smell it, Tom?" he asked me. "Christ, Tom, can you not smell?"

We went back out into the air. Askew spat, cleared his throat, spat again. I peered south, watching for him, expecting him. "He'll be coming," I said. Askew was stamping the earth, beating his foot regularly into the sand. "Yes," he told me. "Yes. I know." Suddenly he reached forward and turned my face towards his. "We've got to do something," he said. "We can't let him just go on like this." "Like what?" I answered, but he ignored me and knelt in the sand outside the doorway. He smoothed the sand with his palm, began writing in it. NO TRAMPS ALLOWED HERE. NO ANIMALS. "That's what he is, Tom," he said as I pulled him away. "A bloody beast."

On the way back we kept to the beach. It seemed to take an age. The tide was coming in, massive waves were crashing on the rocks. Now it was I who walked quickly, wanting to be away from here and into the safety of our own bay. We were almost at the pines when we saw him coming through, and I gasped, "Askew!" But Askew simply came to a halt, and stood his ground as the man approached then passed within ten yards of us. For a second he turned to us, tilting his head back in order to peer through his tangled hair, and then continued, climbing up into the dunes, not looking back. "Oh, Christ," whispered Askew, with his voice trembling, and all the way to my door he was filled with excitement, cursing, drumming his fists on his hips, telling me, "We'll get him now, Tom. We'll get the bugger now."

At the gate he held me. He gazed deep into my eyes.

"Daniel!" he whispered.

"Daniel?" I said.

"The little girly boy. He'll get the bugger going. He'll bring him down."

Inside the house, my father and I hurried our meal. "Been far?" he asked me, and I shook my head.

"The beach," I said, and he told me to hurry, to go and change. "We saw the tramp again," I said.

He was fiddling with the buttons of the TV.

"Go on," he said. "Please."

"Have you smelt him?" I said.

"Smelt him? Smelt what? Do it, son. Please."

I washed and changed quickly. I took a moment to stare into the dusk, right back to where the hut was. I shivered, imagined the man reading the sand. Downstairs, father switched off the television. "Tom!" he yelled.

We ran side by side to the square, climbed into the empty bus. As we set off, he shook his head.

"Cuba!" he said. "Bloody Cuba!"

I stared at him.

"Cuba. It's where they're starting it."

We spent all morning preparing for her. I soaped the window frame and the door. I stretched full length beneath the bed, seeking dust and dirt. He pulled off the covers, polished the metal bedhead and bedfoot, fiercely brushed the mattress, and together we lay starched white sheets across the bed, wrapped plump pillows in starched white cases. I ran out, brought in the year's last campions, white from the ground above the beach, red from beneath the garden hedges. "We'll have to be so careful with her, Tom," he said, "So gentle," and he inspected his hands as if they might be clumsy with her, as if they might harm her. He emptied her wardrobe, began re-folding her things, and out of them fell her photograph to the floor, and she lay there looking up at us through the blisters and the cracks, ever-smiling. He let me take it, watched as I slipped it into my shirt pocket, whispered, "That's right, Tom. Keep her safe."

I couldn't settle. Downstairs, I kept returning to the window, watching the lane. "It'll be ages yet," he told me. "Go on out. Walk some of that energy away." Out there, I prowled a narrow patch of the beach, my senses all alert for her. Daniel came, and he was filled with the coming war. "Look," he said, kneeling in the sand, drawing with a dried-out piece of driftwood, "This is where the bloody Yanks are, circling Cuba. These are the Russians, coming in. They won't turn back, Tom. Not now. Not after all they've said." He took hold of my arm. "There's nothing we can do. A few more days and it could all be over. Nothing left. Tom?"

I'd turned away from him to face the lane.

"She's coming home today," I said, and he cursed and stepped closer to me, put his arms around me. I let him hold me and he whispered, "She must be better, Tom. She must be well." He waited with me for an hour or more, and he kept attending to me with words of reassurance, setting up games for us - tossing stones at debris, making pictures in the sand - but all the time he kept turning his eyes towards the sky, scanning the horizon. "It's how it'll start," he said. "Suddenly. No warning." Then he left me, whispering, "Take care," as Askew came along the shore.

"Aye," said Askew, mocking him, "He knows there's something up. You didn't tell him, Tom? Good lad, good mate." I shuffled back towards the house. "It'll do no harm, you know," he said. "We get Daniel there.The beast thinks he's beautiful. He can't control himself. He attacks. We're the witnesses, Tom. Whatever happens, we tell the tale. And they have to do something, have to get rid of him. "

I clenched my fists.

"But why should Daniel do it?" I said.

"Why? Because we'll fucking make him, mate."

"Oh, Askew," I groaned, at the same time seeing the ambulance behind him coming along the lane and I stood stockstill, hearing nothing more that Askew said, while they opened the doors and carried her in.

"She's home," I whispered. "Let me go." And he turned round in surprise.

"That's great," he said. "You'll be your old self again now."

She was already in the bed, and she composed a teasing smile for me as I walked in, but her face was pale as the white campions, her eyes as bruised as the red. Soon her features settled back into exhaustion, and we crouched on either side of her, linked arms across the tiny ridge of her body. "It'll be so much better now," she whispered. "It'll be just like it was."

"Yes," I whispered, wanting to feed her, to nourish her, to bring her back to bloom, but within minutes she was sleeping, hardly breathing.

That night I kept staring from my bed towards the stars. I listened, but there were only the gentle waves, my father snoring. Then I heard her groans, and I dreamed again of being on starched sheets with her. She was suddenly huge, swollen with life. I delivered the child for her, and when I placed it in the space between us, I saw that it was she who was the child. I lifted her again, left the husk of her body on the bed. I ran into the night, splashed on the tideline, giggling and free, yelling Australia!, feeling her in my arms and her long curls dancing at my throat.

When I woke, the sun was streaming in at the window. The tide was far out, the sky was featureless, the whole world was still. I padded across the landing, peeped in at their door, saw her twisted at the bed's foot, sleeping, gasping for air. Downstairs I found my father in the kitchen. He leaned forward at the sink, gripping its edge. He didn't turn. "Oh, my God, Tom," he said, his voice deeper than it had ever been. "Oh, Tom." Then he growled and I looked out, saw the tramp coming in at our gate. "Today?" I said. "The beast? The bloody beast?" And I grabbed a kitchen knife, threw the door open, stepped out at him. "No tramps!" I said, pointing the knife to his head. "You understand? No tramps here!" He tilted his head back and turned his empty gaze into my eyes. "No!" I said. "Not here. No animals here." And as he left I flung the knife uselessly towards the sea, heard it rattling the weeds beyond the lane.

I drew my father away from the sink. "She will be fine," I told him. "It's up to us. We'll do it. We'll make her like she was."

I went back up with him and we woke her. He lifted her from the awful bed and went to bathe her. Hardly able to breathe, I stripped off yesterday's sheets. I'd returned with fresh ones when he carried her back in. She was humming Beatles tunes, her eyes were shining, and she whispered, "Won't it be lovely, my Tom, once we're free of all this?"

It was early afternoon. The coal gatherers had come down and they stood in the waves, sifting the sand. I sat watching the familiar rise and fall of the water. I gazed north towards the lighthouse, south towards the docks. I understood her now: this was a narrow, constraining place. The same landscape, same faces. When Daniel came I simply let him sit with me, let him talk of the immense sky. "You won't see them," he told me. "But you can't stop yourself from watching for them. It'll mean the end of all of this." Even when Askew came, and I found myself sitting between them, Daniel stayed. "There's nothing to do now," he had said. "Nowhere to go." I could feel Askew burning. In the moments he was silent, I took out her photograph, held it cupped in my palms. Then he started. "I saw him," he said. "He was in beside the fountain. He had his hands full of fucking bread, a big bottle of tea. I shouted at him. Tramp! I shouted, Bloody tramp! He didn't even turn a hair. Wait'll he sees what we've got waiting. You hear that, girly? You hear that, pretty girl?" Daniel didn't move, didn't speak. Askew leaned over me, gripped Daniel's thigh. "Such pretty legs," he growled. "Such pretty cheeks. You'll get the beast rising." I stood up and pushed them apart. "Askew!" I said. But it was too late. The tramp had entered the lane. "Tramp!" yelled Askew. "Beast! Look what we've laid out for you." And he squatted over Daniel, spread him like a sacrifice upon the beach. "Wouldn't you like this lovely girly boy?" he roared. It made the tramp dead still. He stood before the house and he stared down at us, as if willing us to see the true depths of his exhaustion. Then he turned his face towards the empty sky, opened the red gash of his mouth, and truly like an animal began to howl.

Afterwards, in the silence, Daniel was free. Askew knelt stupidly in the sand, over nothing. The coal gatherers and their ponies had turned to us in wonder. I gripped the photograph, held it tight in my fist. Nothing but the sea moved. There seemed nothing left, but then there came my father, in excitement, yelling from inside,

"Tom...! Tom...! Oh,Tom...!"

# David Almond

David Almond's stories have been widely published, and broadcast on Radio 4. He edited the influential fiction magazine, *Panurge*, for six years until 1993. He has won many prizes and awards, including a Hawthornden Fellowship for 1997. This is his second collection of stories. The first collection, *Sleepless Nights*, is also published by IRON Press. He lives in Newcastle upon Tyne.

*author photograph: Claire McNamee*

## IRON Press